UNINTENDED CONSEQUENCES

A collection of speculative fiction tales

DAVID A. WIMSETT

Cape Split Press

TM

Nova Scotia, Canada
https://www.capesplitpress.com
Published by arrangement with the author

ISBN 978-1-990720-02-4

Cover image© BiancoBlue | Dreamstime.com
Clouds and moon © Stanislav Rykunov | Dreamstime.com
Men in outline © Tonitoon | Dreamstime.com
Martian Colony © Algol | Dreamstime.com
Cavern © Grandfailure | Dreamstime.com
Crystal © Ritthichai Wisetchat | Dreamstime.com

Use under licensed agreements with the artists

The Hell of It originally appeared in Askance Magazine
Time and Tide originally appeared in The Absent Willow Review
Something on My Mind was originally published as a novella

Extraordinary Worlds
filled with promise and dread

Triple Winner at The BookFest Awards

Gold medal for Robots, Computers & AI
Gold medal for Space Exploration
Silver medal for Sci-Fi Crime & Mystery

Internationally award-winning author David A. Wimsett examines the consequences of human actions in this collection of five speculative fiction stories.

Children of a space colony question the home their parents chose for them before they were born.

A powerful executive wakes up in hell to find fire and brimstone replaced with modern cities and unending opportunities, or so it seems.

A scientist discovers the secret of time travel and its challenges.

In a future world where AI robots provide all goods and services and people can meet anyone instantly through virtual spaces with no need for physical contact, a police detective uncovers a conspiracy, but not the one he expected.

A young man's quest for a magical dagger takes on new meaning when he meets an aged wizard.

Each tale follows characters as they reach crises in their lives that can change their futures for good or ill

Other Books by David A. Wimsett

THE CARANDIR SAGA
Dragons Unremembered
Volume I

In a multicultural world of gender equality, the monarchs of Carandir work together to prevent sorcerers from waking an evil dragon while rival baronies plot civil war.

Half Awakened Dreams
Volume II

The king is captured by a former lover who reveals the son he unknowingly fathered, the heir to the crown who vows to kill the king. Only the queen can rescue him as exiled nobles return to seize their former lands and begin to suppress women and drive minorities out in a civil war.

Covenant with the Dragons
Volume III

The evil dragon prepares to wake. Civil war rages. Missions to seek aid from allies are thwarted. A princess born far from the strife is tempered to return and face the evils.

BEYOND THE SHALLOW BANK

Artist Margaret Talbot suffers a life changing crisis and comes to a small fishing village where she meets many people, one of whom is a young woman rumored to be a selkie from Celtic mythology. With the influence of the villagers and her own self-determination, Margaret strives to discover who she is and what she truly wants.

To the memory of Ernest Dust

English teacher extraordinaire

Acknowledgments

I owe deep thanks to my editor, Nancy Cassidy, who helped me polish the prose and to Ann, who spotted those unintended inconsistencies every writer overlooks.

David A. Wimsett

June, 2024

The Old Country

The water purification and sanitary reclamation unit sat thirty meters below the Martian surface to shield it from the bombardment of solar and cosmic radiation. As such, it was located in the deepest part of the colony. Most of the operations were automated. Narrow maintenance corridors ran between pipes and stainless-steel tanks. Except for yearly inspections, they were left in darkness as they had been most of the time over the two decades since their initial construction by the first colonists from Earth. It was one of the few areas in the underground complex where there were no security cameras.

Kamille Boro felt along the railing of a catwalk in the darkness between the main effluent intake and the first settling chamber. She was twenty-one by the reckoning of Earth years but her official age was recorded as eleven when calculated by the Martian year that was equivalent to six hundred eighty-seven Earth days.

No one could have seen her black skin or tall, slender frame in the lightless unit. The whirl of motors echoed in the background. She counted her steps toward the designated point as she listened for the sound of another person. Her right hand came upon a small scratch in the railing and she halted.

She tapped on the rail twice with the shank of a screwdriver. A dull thud cut through the silence in the darkness.

She waited two more heartbeats before she gave a single tap.

The whisper of Tim Collins came to one ear. "Did you find the extra fuel canister I left in the lander?"

She couldn't see his pale, white skin that would not take on any color, even under the artificial sun lamps beneath the ground.

She reached out and felt Tim's arm. "Yes." Her voice was almost inaudible. "No one will find it before the next inspection launch."

Tim pressed an eduvisor into her hands. "I found a cognaexperience hidden in a drawer in Dr. Klem's room when I cleaned up for him yesterday."

She fitted the skull cap over her short cut, Afro-textured hair. The sensors pulsed low power signals into the areas in her brain that collected and interpreted the information from her senses; sight, sound, taste, smell and touch.

The darkness was replaced with a scene of something nearly incomprehensible; a plane of seemingly unending water that rushed up to cover the ground she stood on. A roar came with the movement. She feared it would pick her up and drag her beneath even though the rational part of her mind told her it was only an illusion. Still, she took a step back, opened her mouth and gave a quiet, "Oh."

Tim whispered, "Shh."

She pulled the eduvisor from her head with a gasp. "What was that?"

"An ocean on Earth."

She slowed her breathing. Gradually, she placed the eduvisor back on. It was still a shock to see so much water in one place. Above the ocean was a bright, blue sky with something she had only read about—clouds.

A sandy beach ran along the shore. Next to it was a stand of trees.

There were only eight stunted trees in the central park atrium of the colony. They grew under a lead impregnated, glass dome where sunlight seeped through from the pale Martian atmosphere.

Before her were dozens, perhaps hundreds of trees.

The shortest was three times her height.

Her throat tightened as tears fell down her face. "It's so beautiful. I never imagined. How could I?"

She felt Tim take her hands. "I cried, too, when I first saw it."

Kamille removed the eduvisor and sniffled. "That's where we belong, not crawling underground on a dead world."

Tim took the eduvisor back. "We will, Kamille, no matter what the elders say."

Communication between Earth and the colony was relayed through the orbiting spaceship the colonists arrived in.

They needed no supplies from their former planet. Oxygen, minerals and water buried beneath the Martian surface for billions of years were tapped into. Hydroponic gardens provided ample food. All waste was recycled

The spacecraft required fuel to maintain its orbit. This was supplied by the lander used by the members of the original expedition to the surface. Supply missions rocketed off the Martian surface at dawn five times a Martian year and returned two days later.

A consortium effort of private investors financed the expedition. Candidates were screened from thousands of applicants for physical and mental health.

For two years preceding the landing, rockets sent containers filled with building materials to construct domed dwellings on the surface along with vehicles, organic material for hydroponic gardens and equipment to extract, purify and recycle the ancient water of Mars.

Over the next two years, sixty-one babies were born, thirty-two girls and twenty-nine boys until the pregnancies stopped abruptly.

The colonists were baffled. It took years before they could analyze enough data to realize the domed structures were inadequate to protect them from cosmic radiation and solar winds as they slammed through the thin atmosphere of Mars with its nonexistent magnetic field. The bombardment of radiation over years left every adult sterile. Cancer of the lungs, liver and brain were discovered in twelve of them. Six died before the end of the next Martian year.

Work began on a dwelling beneath the soil. The first underground habitation was crude and cramped. The complex expanded to accommodate all the survivors and their children over the intervening decades with apartments, work spaces, education facilities, utility areas and parks. Leaded glass domes were placed over three parks near the surface on the first level. Artificial lights illuminated the rest of the colony. These were powered by a field of solar collectors whose surfaces had to be constantly cleared of dust.

Original colonists continued to develop cancer. Eighty-one had died since the landing. To safeguard against more radiation exposure, eggs and sperm of the children who had not been exposed as long were harvested and placed in frozen storage as a backup in case those offspring became sterile as they aged.

Kamille was one of the last children born on Mars. She and the other young women moved underground in infancy were scheduled to bear the next generation through a program set out by the elders to ensure the best genetic results.

She began pilot training with ground school and

simulator time when she was nine Martian years old. At ten she took her first flight and soon became a co-pilot. After five missions in the lander, she was ready to take command.

The co-pilot on her first mission as captain was her instructor, George Simms. They wore spacesuits, helmets and gloves. She strapped herself in the prone position of the Captain's chair.

Through the forward view port, she watched as the heavy doors protecting the hanger bay from the Martian atmosphere opened to reveal the pale, orange sky of dawn. The metal launch pad with the lander positioned on it rose to the surface.

She inspected a gauge. "Fuel pressure normal."

"Fuel pressure normal," echoed Simms.

"Ignition sequence primed."

"Ignition sequence primed."

"Ignition in three, two, one." She touched a button on the display console.

The rocket motors fired smoothly.

Four seconds later she said, "Release docking clamps."

"Docking clamps released."

The gravity, thirty-eight percent of that on Earth, required a fraction of the fuel a rocket would need on Earth to gain orbit. The engines burned hydrogen and oxygen extracted from the Martian soil and held in canisters stored in underground vaults.

When they achieved orbit, Kamille maneuvered the craft for rendezvous. They circled Mars three times before they saw the massive tubular space craft the colonists from Earth traveled in to reach the red planet.

Kamille had docked the lander many times in the

simulator. She kept a calm outer posture, but her heart pounded in her chest as they approached.

Simms remained silent, though his hands were near the co-pilot's controls.

Kamille lined up the sites and adjusted the thrusters. "Fifty meters."

"Fifty meters, Captain."

"Engage laser sighting."

"Laser sighting engaged."

"Twenty meters. Open docking pins."

"Docking pins open."

"Ten meters. Five, three, one."

There was a slight jar. Kamille let out a sigh. "Secure docking pins."

"Docking pins secure." Simms smiled. "Good docking, Captain."

"Thank you. Depressurize the cabin,"

Even through her space helmet, she heard the hiss of oxygen as it was pumped into storage cylinders.

Kamille waited until the air pressure gauge read zero. "Make ready for fuel transfer."

"Fuel lines engaged."

"Begin refueling."

"Refueling underway."

"Open the airlock hatch and prepare for inspection."

"Hatch open."

The fuel transfer could have been performed from ground control, but each refueling also involved an inspection with any required maintenance of the systems.

They entered the airlock and opened a second hatch to the habitable areas of the orbiter. During the journey from Earth, it spun on its axis to create low, artificial gravity within walls shielded with reinforced polyethylene with a high hydrogen content to absorb and disperse radiation and protect the people inside for the months required to reach Mars.

The cylinder's spin was turned off after the colonists descended to the Martian surface. The last crew members to leave strung lines along its length and down to key stations to move around in zero gravity. The air recyclers were also disabled and the oxygen stored under pressure in tanks. Crews were required to wear spacesuits.

Everything was kept in pristine working condition, not only to maintain communication with Earth but, to serve as a lifeboat in case of a crisis on the surface until the problem was resolved.

It was always a thrill to enter the cavernous area in zero gravity. The first few times, Kamille let herself fly across the space like a child sledding down a hill, though she had experienced neither snow nor sledding. Simms and the other pilots let her play for a moment before they called her back to duty.

This time, she moved with grace and dignity as she and Simms checked instrument readouts and looked for signs of wear or hull breach. The crew area once accommodated nearly two hundred people with control rooms, food preparation areas, recreation space, sleeping quarters and storage.

Simms held a pad. "Which checklist do you want me to go through, Captain?"

Kamille paused, then laughed. "Oh, yes. I forgot. I'm the one in charge. I'll start with the com links. You can check the shielding between the outer hull and the habitat."

"Very good."

Simms pulled himself along a line to the far side of the cylinder, then opened a hatch and floated inside.

Kamille started the self-diagnostic routine in the communications software. Once it began to run, she returned to the lander and opened a storage locker. Inside was the extra fuel canister Tim had loaded along with a dozen packets of freeze-dried food. She moved the cylinder through the airlock and secured it in a storage bin. Then, she returned and placed the food in the same bin.

Simms called over the radio. "Inspection complete, captain. No punctures or deterioration."

"Acknowledged. I'm just about finished with the com systems. Return to the cylinder and complete your check list."

They entered the lander six hours later, repressurized it, and ate a meal. After a rest period, they undocked.

Kamille brought the lander back to the pad. It was lowered beneath the surface and the door to the underground hanger closed.

Simms turned to Kamille and nodded. "Congratulations, Captain. You are now a fully qualified pilot."

She grinned. "Thank you." Then, guilt flooded her at the realization this and other trips had secretly prepared the spacecraft to depart Mars when she, and all those born on the red planet, would betray their parents and return to Earth.

Harvey Tian and Amara Biker had worked in the fuel production plant since they were fifteen. Harvey earned a chemical engineering degree and Biker was nearing the end of her studies in an accelerated course of education that lasted eight and a half hours a day, five days a week with only six holiday breaks. The two of them often met Kamille and Tim in a park on the third level under the surface for dinner and a game of backgammon or cards in the evenings.

It was a public place used by few people as it had no fountains or trees. Like most of the colony, surveillance cameras fed images to computers that looked for anyone in distress so medical teams could be dispatched quickly. The cameras also picked up sound. Teams of emergency responders watched live feeds from random cameras while the computer analyzed all movement.

They ate over a game of gin rummy.

Tim winked at Kamille. "Congratulations on your first command. It must have been a thrill."

She dealt the cards. "It was."

"Did you accomplish everything you planned on doing?"

"Yes. I had to work hard but I got everything done."

Amara picked up her cards. "You're always a hard worker Kam. I imagine George Simms has never caught you napping."

"I've never been accused of that."

Harvey led. "We've been busy as well. A lot of people are depending on us but we managed to keep a little reserve of energy to ensure we meet our quota."

Tim said, "Are there any problems with production? I'll be loading fuel tomorrow."

"We're right on schedule." said Amara.

"That's good," said Tim. "We certainly don't want to let the others down. Kamille wouldn't want to run out of juice."

Kamille smiled. "I'm so glad that I have such good friends to count on."

Harvey laid down a card. "Everyone's counting on us."

During the next five flights, Kamille took command as captain three times. She always assigned George Simms to inspect the hull, saying that he was more experienced, while she transferred extra fuel and food to the orbiter.

One night Harvey didn't show up at the park. Amara said he had been transferred to help design some new flow regulators for the hydroponic gardens. Kamille saw the worry in the young woman's face but asked no further questions.

The next day Kamille performed her routine inspection of the lander. Simms had not arrived. She peeked into the storage locker where Tim always left the fuel canister. It was empty.

Kamille used the exercise room on the third floor near her quarters. She panted as she ran on a treadmill.

Councilor Rita Hou walked in and mounted a stationary bicycle. "George Simms said you did very well on your first flight as captain."

The hair on the back of Kamille's neck stood up. Hou was one of the elders who sat on the council. She worked on the first level with all the other councilors. The exercise area there had a pool and sauna with weights and several treadmills and bicycles.

Hou adjusted the tension on her stationary bike. "I understand your friend Amara Biker will get her degree soon. She's very bright with many good ideas."

Kamille fought to keep her voice calm. "Yes, she'd be honored to know you feel that way."

"Well, she worked quite closely with Harvey Tian before his transfer. He's quite resourceful."

Kamille said nothing.

Hou got off the bike and wiped her neck with a towel. "Your friends are all very clever young people; Tim Collins, William Fisk, Mary Owens and so many others."

Kamille stopped running. She was breathing hard and hoped Hou would think that was just from the exercise.

The councilor formed a crooked smile. "I need your help. Would you come with me to the council chambers?"

Kamille followed Hou to the first level. They came to the doors of the council room.

Hou opened them. "Step inside."

The council chamber was an audience hall. It could accommodate three dozen spectators, yet the gallery was empty.

Seven people sat at a raised, curved bench at the front. Above them was one of the domes through which the Martian sky could be seen. Chairs were placed just in front of the bench. Kamille recognized nine of the conspirators who intended to return to Earth sat in them. Harvey Chen was not among them.

Dr. Brimmer, the head of the council, indicated a chair in front of the bench.

Kamille looked around the room before she took the seat.

Councilor Elizabeth Schuller stood and cast a glance at the young people. "Did you really think no one would notice the extra fuel production or the food missing from stores?" She sat back in her chair. "Harvey Tian has been subjected to physical and chemical interrogation. We hoped we would never have to do such a thing, but we had to have the truth. We know everything about your plans to return to Earth."

Another councilor shook his head. "Why? Why do you betray our trust? We've given you everything and this is how you treat us?"

None of the young people spoke.

After a long silence, Dr. Brimmer sighed. "We came

here to open up a new world. This is your home. You don't understand what Earth is or why we left. It was not only for adventure and scientific research. Those are important to us, yet we left a place that was corrupt to establish a new land of equality and kindness. We keep track of the doings of our former planet. The greed and hate and wars have only become worse. Why would you want to leave a land of peace for that?"

Councilor Rachel Smith looked pained. "You are the first generation we gave life to, the first Martians. That's why we came and sacrificed and why some of us died, so we can step above our base instincts and ensure the survival of the human race. Haven't you learned anything about compassion? We live in harmony with different colors and backgrounds. Have we taught you nothing?"

Kamille grasped the arm of her chair as glared at the elders. Her voice was faint. "We didn't ask to be here."

Councilor Smith returned Kamille's gaze. "People have migrated to new lands for millennia. How could we ask those who were not born and never knew the strife we fled from?"

Tim leapt to his feet and jabbed his finger toward Smith. "That was your vision. We never had a chance to vote. You brought us into a world without oceans, grass, clouds or the ability to walk outside of a secluded colony without a spacesuit. We've been robbed of this."

His father, Councilor James Collins, shook his head. "I never thought I'd hear such from my own son. You've been given opportunities few on Earth have for an education that surpasses any university and the opportunity to use that education to explore an entire world."

"To what end? We're forced to exist in a tiny, stagnant society. We see the same people every day because there have been no children in over two decades."

"Every new colony starts off small, son. We'll grow. You'll bear the next generation of true Martians. There'll be hundreds more, then thousands."

Amar shook her head. "There will be no offspring."

Kamille stood, her face a calm mask. "All of us, your children, have spent unsupervised time on duty to clean the solar arrays. Each of us has entered the abandoned domes and removed our spacesuits to become sterile like you. It's something everyone born on Mars agreed to do long ago. None of us can conceive children."

The room became silent as the councilors looked to one another.

Councilor Collins stood. "Son, this can't be true."

"Yes father, it is. We will not condemn another generation to grow up in this dead place against their will"

Dr. Brimmer's voice echoed in the chambers. "You insolent brats. Enough of your eggs and sperm are stored safely away. If need be, each young woman will be artificially inseminated and held until she gives birth. We have failed with you, but we will raise your offspring to respect our goals."

Kamille's voice was quiet. "When did you last check the cryogenic canisters? Samuel Kemp built a feedback loop to show a consistent temperature on the dials before he turned the refrigerant off. Those eggs and sperm are dead."

Dr. Brimmer exploded in fury. "There will be no more discussion. You have been led astray by fantasy. Not all of you could have been exposed long enough to be sterile."

He sat back in his chair and took several deep breaths. "You are still young and youth, by nature, will rebel to assert itself. Over time you will see the wisdom of the course we have set you on. As you mature, reality will change your minds. Until then you will be watched and monitored. Go back to your duties. We will not speak of this again."

Kamille remained standing steadfast before the council. "You can't watch every one of us all the time."

James Collins said, "You can't leave without a lander. We'll destroy it if we have to."

"Even if you do," said Kamille, "We possess the knowledge to build a new one if we have to cannibalize everything in this colony. How many elders have died of cancer already? How long will it be before you don't have the physical strength to restrain us? Ten years?—twenty? Time is on our side. It will parole us, no matter what you do."

She held her gaze stern as the councilors wept.

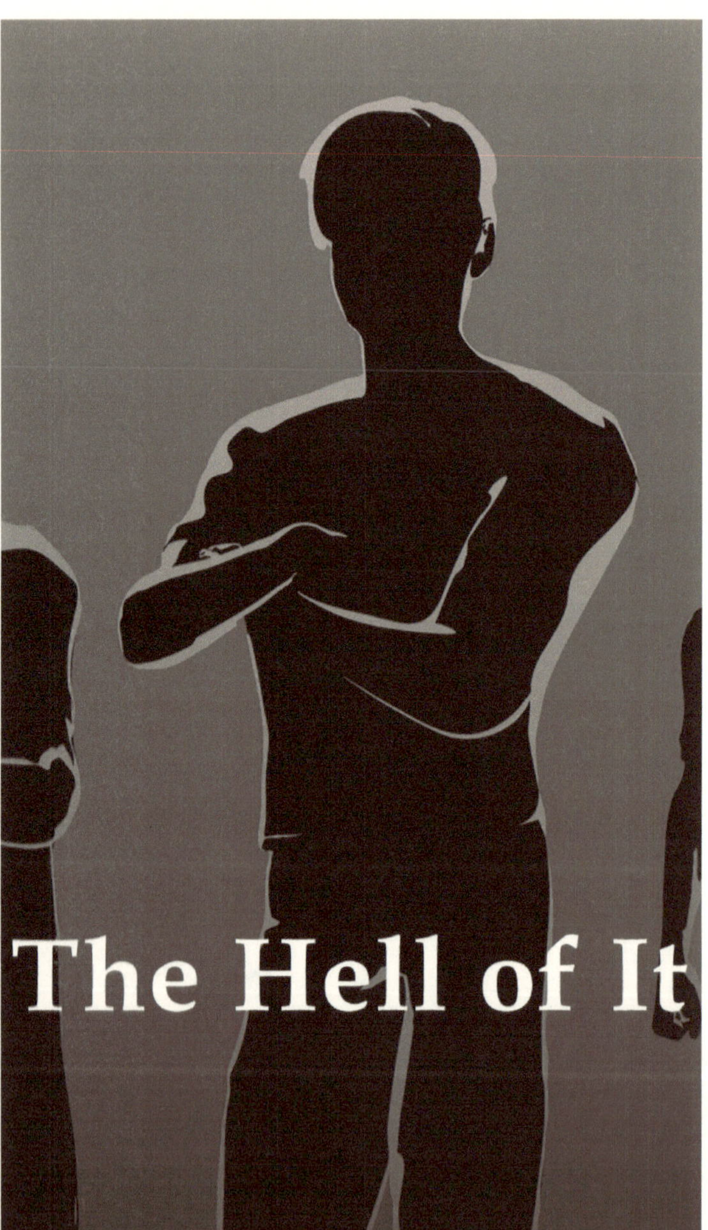

The Hell of It

The single lamp in the small office was lowered to the desk so it only illuminated the ledger Mary Jones altered. She heard the door open and looked up to see a man standing at the threshold silhouetted against the glare of the hallway light.

She quickly covered the paper with her hand. "Oh, Mr. Ferguson. I thought you were finished with the audit."

Ferguson entered the office. "I have just one more thing to clear up."

"What is that?"

He walked up to the desk and moved Mary's hand away from the ledger. "The money you've embezzled from the firm over the last eight months."

Mary pulled her hand away. "I don't know what you mean."

"The entries were well done. I might not have caught your crime if I hadn't found one receipt dropped behind a filing cabinet."

"You don't understand. It's just a loan. Mr. Wells approved the transfers."

"He never mentioned it in any interviews." He took out his phone. "I'll give him a call."

Mary pulled a side drawer of the desk open, grabbed a pistol and stood. "Hang up."

"Would you add murder to embezzlement?"

"You don't understand. I just need a little money to start my own advertising company. I'll pay it back, every cent. I just can't get a bank loan right now."

"You could have asked Mr. Wells."

Mary gave a short snort. "Ask for a loan to go into competition?" She panted as sweat rolled down her face. "Look. I've got more than I need. Forget you ever found that receipt and I'll make it worth your while."

Ferguson advanced on her. "I don't take bribes. Hand me that gun."

Mary's hand shook violently. Her finger jerked in a spasm. The gun fired. She closed her eyes and recoiled from the shock of the blast. When she looked again, Ferguson lay face down on floor.

She dropped the gun. "Oh God. No." She bent down. "I didn't mean to fire. I'll call an ambulance." She turned him on his side and stared into his lifeless eyes, then dropped his body and covered her face with her hands.

Her mind raced. She removed his wallet and watch, then turned the auditor's body on its back and dragged it by the heels to the alley behind the office. It would seem like just another unsolved robbery. No one would suspect her. There was a moment of regret and guilt. These passed quickly as she realized her dream of opening her own advertising agency was secure.

She used the stolen money to start that agency and hired bright, young minds to staff it. Still, she held the reins of power tightly as she controlled everyone and placed her mark on each deal.

After decades of lying, bullying and cheating, a stroke felled her. When she returned to the office, it was evident some of her power had slipped away. A purge of dissident subordinates returned her to full control, but a second stroke put her in intensive care.

As she woke in a hospital bed, her eyesight blurry, muffled noises came quivering through a haze. She tried to speak. No words came out. Someone started to laugh in a deep and unpleasant tone. She closed her eyes and drifted into darkness.

When Mary opened her eyes, she sat in an office chair.

Plush carpet covered the floor.

A potted tree occupied one corner.

To her left, a wide window showed fluffy clouds against a bright blue sky.

The air was a pleasant temperature with the dry sense of central air conditioning.

In front of her, a tall, clean-shaven man in a tailored suit sat at a desk.

The man stood and extended his hand as he walked forward. "Welcome Ms. Jones. Welcome to Hell."

She returned his firm handshake. "I beg your pardon."

He smiled pleasantly. "You're probably a little disoriented at the moment. Now, what I'm about to say may distress you, but please be assured everything is just fine.

"A moment ago, you were lying in a hospital bed suffering from a stroke. You died as a result. At that exact instant, your soul materialized here in the afterlife."

Mary looked at her hands and realized her eyesight, blurry only moments ago, was now clear and sharp. The age spots and wrinkles on her skin were gone, as was the hospital gown. Instead, she was dressed in the same red business suit she wore the day she opened her own advertising agency. She got to her feet and examined herself in a mirror on the wall. Her grey hair was dark auburn again.

She saw the face of the tall man reflected behind her. He was still smiling. "As fine a figure as ever you were at thirty-four. I believe that was your favorite age."

Mary ran her hands across the fabric. "I threw this out years ago. How is this possible, mister…"? She paused for a moment. "I'm sorry. I didn't catch your name."

"Satan. Beelzebub Satan. But please, call be Beel."

The skin on the back of her neck prickled. "It's the

drugs, that's it. What did that doctor give me?" The prickling feeling continued. She took in ragged, short breaths. All the sermons of hellfire and torment she heard as a child flooded her mind. "I didn't mean to kill him. It was an accident. You have to believe me."

Satan raised his hand. "Calm yourself, Mary. All that fire and brimstone nonsense has nothing to do with Hell. We know about the money you stole, the people you cheated, the careers you ruined, even the man you killed. That doesn't matter. Good deeds. Bad deeds. They all wash in the end. Hell wasn't created to punish those who sin." He chuckled. "If it were, everyone would wind up here. No, Hell is just a place where certain kinds of souls come, those with the drive to make it. For some there is heaven, for others Hell. Or to put it another way, the sheep have their pasture and the wolves their forest."

Mary took a step away from Satan. "Then, what happens to me here?"

Satan spread his arms wide. "What would you like to happen? It's a whole new world waiting to be conquered, waiting for people who know how to make their mark and keep it there. Name your game; banking, shipping, media. It's all here, and more. Oh, it won't be easy. But I can assure you it will never be dull. Wouldn't that be the worst? To be bored through eternity."

Mary walked to the window. Outside, she saw a modern city with a meandering river running through it. In the distance tree lined mountains were topped with snow. She turned back to Satan. "But what do you get out of it? What's your cut, Beel?"

"Let's just say I'm the CEO of a multidimensional conglomerate. You make a profit and I make a profit, but not in dollars and cents. There are other things to strive for."

"So, it's like a contest between you and..." She looked up at the ceiling, "God?"

"Something like that, only I wouldn't gaze in that direction. Heaven is off there to the west. Very pastoral, but a little too sedate for my taste."

"Harps and halos?"

"No, but new arrivals do wear the most awful white robes and they're set to the same age as when they died. God says it helps them acclimatize. I think you'll agree setting people to their favorite age is much better, especially since you can change whenever you want."

"Do you mean I can trade this body in for a new one?"

"Not exactly. The body you have now is the one you will keep for as long as you are in Hell. We can alter it if you like or repair it if it gets hurt, but we can't replace it if it's destroyed. When you die here, Mary, your soul has nowhere to go. It just vanishes into oblivion."

He opened a drawer and brought out a metal box. "But, don't let that worry you. For now, just have a look around, get used to the place." He took out a set of keys and a small handbag. "Here's some cash and a few credit cards. They'll get you going. The square key is to your apartment, the address is in the wallet, and the round one is for..."

"My Matla Turbo. Is it really my car?"

Satan smiled broadly. "Red with wire rim wheels, sun roof and leather seats."

She took the keys and handbag. "I can't believe it. It's everything I loved best."

"We've opened a small advertising agency for you downtown. It's not much, a couple of accounts, a little working capital, some employees, but then, you started with less, didn't you?"

"I certainly did."

Satan guided her to his outer office. "If you have any problems just call. My secretary will give you the number. We'll talk again in a few weeks. Good luck."

The apartment was a modern set of rooms built into the shell of a Victorian building. Her favorite clothes hung neatly in a closet. The kitchen cabinets were full of food. Her grandmother's chinaware shone from a lighted display case. Everything was right.

The drive downtown took a quarter of an hour. Her office occupied a two-story brick building. The staff consisted of three advertising agents, a receptionist and a janitor who also filled in as a handyman. Mary sat through a staff meeting to get acquainted with the accounts. She was in control again. The excitement was still there, and this time it would never end.

Business grew over the next year. One night, Mary closed a deal for the largest account her agency had ever landed. The final negotiations lasted well past midnight. She took the staff out for drinks.

One of her employees said, "Congratulations, boss. That was brilliant."

Another one raised a glass in a toast. "You made them squirm all right."

Mary smiled. "It was just good business negotiation, even if it was shooting fish in a barrel."

Everyone laughed.

When she got home, she stumbled into the bedroom, still fully clothed, flopped across the covers, and immediately fell asleep.

She had a dream about a tree-lined avenue. At first, she saw only misty forms. The mist vanished as her senses snapped clearly into focus with shocking reality.

Mary stood in her grandmother's kitchen and stared at the cookie jar just out of reach on top of the refrigerator. She was nine years old.

Grandmother went upstairs for a nap. Mary pushed one of the kitchen chairs over to the refrigerator and reached up for the lid of the cookie jar. She told herself no one would notice if a few were missing. The lid was higher than she thought. She placed her hands around the jar to take it down when it slipped and fell to the floor with a crash.

Grandmother called down, "What's wrong?"

Mary stared at the broken shards of pottery. She opened the back door that led to the driveway between grandmother's house and the next-door neighbors.

Grandmother came downstairs. "What was that noise?"

Mary pointed to the open door, "Jimmy Watson came in and tried to steal some cookies. He dropped the jar when he saw me". She remembered how grandmother always complained about Jimmy and how he made too much noise and cut across her lawn and stomped through her flower beds.

Grandmother got a strange look on her face. "Well, this is the last straw."

Mary knew grandmother would be angry, but she thought she would just complain like she always did and that would be the end of it. Instead, grandmother went over and knocked on the neighbor's door.

The man next door appeared. "Hello Thelma. What can I do for you?"

"That boy of yours came into my kitchen and broke my cookie jar."

"Did you see him?"

"My granddaughter did and she wouldn't lie."

The man looked back into the house. "Jimmy. get out here."

Jimmy Watson appeared at the door. "Yes?"

"Why did you go into Mrs. Jones' kitchen and break her cookie jar?"

"I didn't."

The man grabbed Jimmy by the arm and dragged him inside. "Don't you lie to me."

She heard Jimmy shouting, "No. I didn't do it. Ow. No. Ow."

Later that day, she went outside. Jimmy Watson walked up and stood still as he stared at Mary. She was afraid he was about to hit her and wanted to run, but was too scared to move.

He just lowered his head and said, "Why?"

The single word hurt more than if he had punched her in the stomach.

The nightmare ended as the wail of a siren woke Mary. She sat up with a start, caught for a moment between the dreaming world and the waking. Her clothes were soaked with sweat. She got up and made some instant coffee. Her hands shook as she tried to sip the hot liquid. It had been ages since she thought about the incident of the cookie jar, yet she couldn't stop shaking as she realized a part of her mind waited for Jimmy Watson to come through the door.

The dream was only a distant memory as she drove downtown the next morning. The janitor, Tom, came into her office and emptied her trash.

"Good afternoon, ma'am. Congratulations on closing that deal."

"Thank you, Tom." The janitor appeared to be in his seventies. Mary wondered why he'd set himself at such an age. She shuffled some papers. "We'll have to get you an assistant if business keeps growing."

"Thank you, but I can handle the load. Settling in, are you ma'am?"

"Yes. Hell is a nice place. I took a walk by the lake during lunch and watched the ducks."

Tom dusted a filing cabinet. "Sometimes I feed them bread."

"I'd have remembered to bring some today, if I hadn't been so tired. Couldn't sleep. Had the strangest dream." She looked up.

Tom stared at her, his mouth agape

She sat the papers aside. "What's wrong?"

"Nothing, ma'am."

"You look pale."

"I'm fine ma'am." He left her office in a rush.

The nights the dreams came were terrible. The nights they didn't were almost as bad, as she lay in bed certain they would return. They retraced the petty mistakes, failures and embarrassments of her life; the date who never arrived for the prom, the exam she cheated on, the time she hit the neighbor's cat with her car and hid the body.

The events were always insignificant. She never dreamed about the money she embezzled or the man she killed to cover up the crime. Still, the intensity with which she relived the trivial incidents smothered her.

When she mentioned her dreams, people changed the

subject abruptly, except for Tom. He would stare into her eyes for a moment, then walk away.

She called Satan.

"Stop by your local clinic," he said. "They can give you something."

That night, she took one of the pills and was delighted to awake the next morning free of the nightmares. Business exploded and she threw herself full into work.

A few weeks later she had a dream about her sixteenth birthday when she and her family flew across the country to visit her aunt. There was a shudder. The jet fell several thousand feet. Oxygen masks dropped from the ceiling. As the young Mary grasped hers over her face, she found herself terrified, not so much by death, but by the realization everything she'd ever done amounted to nothing, and no one would remember her name.

When she woke in the apartment, her hands were still over her face.

One morning, she asked Tom to come to the basement with her. "I need some files moved."

They went downstairs where a corridor led to storage rooms. There was a small table with two chairs pushed up underneath it. Across the table top were scattered some papers, two staplers, and a letter opener. A thick layer of dust covered everything.

Tom said. "Is this the right room?"

Mary closed the door. "There are no files. I need to talk to you, alone, about the dreams."

Tom took a step back. "I don't know what you mean."

"You're a poor liar, Tom. I can see it in your face. You have the dreams the same as everyone in Hell."

Tom started to speak, then closed his eyes and bowed

his head.

Mary said, "We can't let this go on."

Tom sat at the table and clasped his hands in front of him. "It won't do any good."

"I need to know what we're fighting."

He gave a sigh. "Yes. Everyone has the nightmares. When I first arrived, I tried to fight them, but they keep coming at you night after night, year after year, every petty blemish of your life. You can stand it for a while, even make them stop for a night or two. You think you can win, if you just hold out. But then, one day, you break." He swept his arm across the table and knocked everything to the floor. "You just break and that's when you know Satan owns you." He put his head in his hands.

Mary touched his shoulder. "How long have you been here?"

He shook his head. "I used to keep track, then it seemed pointless."

"Years?"

He looked up. "Centuries."

She sat in the other chair. "After all that time, you must have learned something about how they make the dreams."

He crossed his arms over his chest. "I once worked in Mr. Satan's building. My body was young then. One day, I stumbled through a door marked Dream Room. There were people inside. Each of them stared into crystal balls. A man passed his hand over one. It glowed and showed a picture of a boy beating a dog with a stick. Then, the dog spun around and bit the boy viciously.

"I gasped. Several people looked up and saw me." Tom closed his eyes tightly. "I don't want to talk about it anymore."

"Tom, it's important. I can stop them from hurting you."

He fell silent for a long while. When he spoke again, his voice was barely audible. "They strapped me in a chair and asked me if I had seen the master crystal and if I knew what it did. They showed me a picture. It was about the size of my fist and bright blue. Mr. Satan came down. He played other peoples' dreams in my mind, over and over. I asked him to stop. I asked nice. Then I begged. Then I screamed.

"Finally, I passed out. When I woke up, I pretended to be asleep. Mr. Satan told someone he had to find out if I knew about the master crystal and how it controlled all the dream makers. They would stop working if the crystal were damaged in any way, even if it just got chipped. That's when Mr. Satan made me this age."

"How did you find this room?"

"It's in a hidden office. The entrance is on the lower level of the parking garage. There's a brass plaque attached to the wall with a crescent moon and three stars on it. You press the stars all together, then the moon twice."

Mary stood. "Take me there."

He shook his head. "If they knew I told you..." His eyes grew frantic. "You don't know what they'll do."

"I can protect you."

He pushed himself up with his eyes glazed over. "I'll go to them and tell the truth. We'll both go."

"Tom, we can fight them together."

"They'll forgive us." He shuffled toward the door.

Mary ran and knocked him to the floor.

He struggled to get up, but was no match for her strength.

Stupid old man, she thought. *He'll ruin everything.*

She tried reason, but he was hysterical. The letter opener Tom knocked from the table was on the floor. *What did Satan say about a soul that died in Hell? It vanished?*

Tom continued to squirm as Mary reached out, grabbed the steel blade, and held it to the old man's throat. "You're not going to spoil this for us, you fool. I want to help you, but if I have to kill you to keep you quiet I will. You know what that means here."

Tom raised his hands over his face. "Please, no. I won't say anything."

He twisted as Mary held the letter opener firmly. His legs jerked up and struck Mary in the back. She fell forward with her full weight. The letter opener rammed into Tom's neck.

Hot blood shot from the wound in spurts. Tom gave a gurgled cough as he opened his eyes wide.

Mary pressed her fingers tight against the gash but only managed to get her clothes soaked in sticky gore.

Tom moved his mouth. No sound came out. His skin began to glow.

Mary jumped back as Tom's body dissolved.

She ran to the other side of the room and vomited. With the sting of bile in her mouth, she whispered, "Oh, God", then realized there was no help for her from that direction. She had to solve this herself, as she solved all her problems so many times before. She would change Hell as she had changed Earth. This time her mark would last for eternity.

The blood was still wet as she drove home. After a shower, she found her only clean outfit was the one she wore when she first arrived in Hell.

No one stopped her as she drove into the underground

garage. The plaque was located in a little niche. She pressed the stars and moon in the right order and a section of wall slid open to reveal a carpeted hallway.

A uniformed guard sat at a desk with his face in a magazine. He wore a belt with a night stick and a side arm. The hallway continued on to a door marked *Dream Room*.

The guard didn't look up. "Badge, please."

Mary stood tall. Her voice was sharp. "Is this how you guard the most important place in Hell? Stand up."

The guard dropped his magazine and stood at attention. "Sorry, ma'am."

She brought her face to within an inch of his. "You should be. What's your number?"

Before the guard could recover his wits, she pulled the gun from his holster and shot him. Like Tom, his skin glowed before his body vanished. She tucked the pistol into the waist band of her suit so the jacket hid it from view. Then, she walked down the hall and through the door.

The dream room stretched before her as thousands of people sat in front of crystal balls where nightmares played out. To the side was a wall with an elevator. Next to it was a large glass window from which a blue glow emanated. Mary walked toward it.

When she reached the window, she saw a silver tripod beyond the glass. On it rested a perfect blue crystal about the size of her fist.

Mary pulled the gun from her waistband, aimed it at the wall of glass and fired. She jumped through the jagged hole the bullet made.

Piercing alarms sounded.

Five uniformed guards charged forward.

Mary grabbed the crystal and pointed the gun at it.

"One more step and I chip this thing."

The guards stopped, then moved back with their hands raised.

Mary looked to one of them. "Dial Satan on that speaker phone."

Satan's voice was calm and measured. "Mary, you must realize what you've done is serious. If you will just hand over the crystal, I'm certain we can come to an agreement."

"Drop the soft sell, Beel. I know what the crystal means. I can bring down your whole operation. No more dreams. No more control. What will that do to your little game with God?"

"Mary, why don't we talk about this? Stay where you are and I'll be down in fifteen minutes."

She was certain she was being set up. If he wanted her there it was the last place she wanted to be. The dream room was the most important place in Hell. He had to have a quick way to get there. She looked to the guard who made the phone call. "How long does it take for your boss to get down here on that elevator?"

"I don't know. A minute or so."

Satan's voice barked through the speakerphone. "Idiot."

Mary smiled. "We'll talk all right, Beel, but not down here. I'm on my way up and remember, I've got a gun pointed at the crystal."

Satan's office was just as she remembered it, the desk, the window, the carpeting. She sat in the same chair with the gun pointed at the master crystal. "Now, Beel. Let's talk."

"I'm listening."

"There are going to be some changes."

"Such as?"

"To begin with, I control who has nightmares and who doesn't."

"That's quite ambitious. Do you plan to hold a lottery, or just take bribes?"

"I don't believe you understand how serious I am."

"Oh, but I do. I've known from the moment you arrived you're a serious woman of action. It's always been that way for you, hasn't it? You have to win; have to make everyone look at you. At first you play by the rules, bending them of course, yet staying within your own interpretation of legal.

"Then something happens that's out of your control. The dreams come, for instance. You try to live with them, but they get worse. You're about to go out of your mind, when you stumble onto an edge. A power crystal can make you master of your tormentors.

"To protect yourself, you kill the person who told you. It's justified. He might tell the authorities Mary Jones knows where the crystal is. One murder leads to another. No real plan but action nonetheless. Of course, you have some regret but not enough to stop you. Then here you are, crystal in hand, demanding your cut of Hell. Very impressive."

Mary felt a growing panic at Satan's relaxed demeanor. "Well, I've got the crystal now, no matter what you say. So, you found out about Tom. So what? Ending his torment was more merciful than what you did to him."

Satan clapped enthusiastically. "Bravo! An excellent rendition of the 'I knew what was best for them' speech. Torquemada, Hitler, Stalin and thousands more have sat in that chair and used those exact words."

"I'm warning you. I'll destroy this crystal."

"Go ahead. It's worthless. Might as well be dust."

With those words, the crystal crumbled into fine blue ash. A breeze came from the air conditioning vents and blew it away. Mary jumped to her feet and aimed the gun at Satan. "You lousy…" She pulled the trigger.

A stick popped out of the barrel and a little flag unfolded with the word BANG written on it in oversized letters.

Satan laughed uproariously as he walked around the desk and took the gun. "Do forgive me. I just can't suppress my love of theatrics." He wiped a tear from his eye as he pressed a button on his phone. "Tom, would you come in here for a moment?"

The door opened and the old janitor Mary stabbed walked into the room. "Hello, ma'am. Nice to see you again."

Satan handed him the gun. "Please take this to props."

"Yes sir." He left and closed the door behind him.

Mary stared with her mouth open. "But I killed him."

"He can't die, Mary. No one here can die."

"But you said a soul killed in Hell would vanish."

Satan shrugged. "I lied."

"Then the guards, the crystal, my office staff?"

"All made up for your benefit."

She sat down slowly. "So, I'll just keep on dreaming about all the petty failures of my life."

Satan raised an eyebrow. "Come now. What kind of torment would that be, really? The nightmares are unpleasant, but not much more than an annoyance. After a few years they would fade into the background the way your conscience did, and there would always be the hope that somehow, some way, you could defeat them. Not much of an eternal punishment, is it?

"No, if you want to find the perfect damnation for a person, you have to know what she really fears, something she's so terrified of she denies it even to herself.

"Imagine someone who has to be in charge; someone who has to control everyone and everything around her so she can secure her legacy. She strives and fights and cheats and destroys anyone in her way until she stands at the pinnacle about to achieve all she has dreamed of.

"Then, at that moment, the dream slips away. She learns everything she's ever done amounts to nothing and she has actually had no effect on the world, as if she had never existed."

Satan's features formed a twisted grimace. "If such a person knew this, even for an instant, it would be the damnation of eternity."

Mary shook as she gasped for air. "What are you talking about?"

Satan sat behind the desk. "In a moment you'll fall asleep. When you wake up, you'll recall nothing of what's happened since your arrival here. The last thing you'll remember will be the hospital where you died."

All strength drained from her arms and legs. Her head felt heavy. She fought to speak. "Please. I have to know. Is this the first time? Have I been through all this before?" Her voice broke into a screech. "How many times have I sat here?"

Satan smiled. "Now that's the hell of it, Mary. You'll never know."

His laughter burned into her mind as she drifted into darkness.

When Mary opened her eyes, she sat in an office chair. Plush carpet covered the floor.

A potted tree occupied one corner.

To her left, a wide window showed fluffy clouds

against a bright blue sky.

The air was a pleasant temperature with the dry sense of central air conditioning.

In front of her, a tall, clean-shaven man in a tailored suit sat at a desk.

The man stood and extended his hand as he walked forward. "Welcome Ms. Jones. Welcome to Hell."

Time

and Tide

D r. Richard Graham charged down the hallway in the psychiatric ward. He was late for his next appointment. With his overwhelming case load, it felt as if he always was.

He entered examination room D.

An eleven-year-old boy sat at a table. He gazed up at a high, barred window whose light cast shadows across his face.

Graham said, "Hello, Frank. Remember me?"

The boy turned his head and stared at the psychiatrist for a moment, then looked back to the window.

Graham glanced at his watch. He was supposed to spend an hour with the boy, but his last appointment ran over, as had the one before that. A group therapy session was set to start in thirty-five minutes. He sat down at the table. "Would you like to talk this time? I want to help you, Frank."

The boy stood and slammed his fist against the table. "Then let me see Dr. Harold Lamont. He's a nuclear physicist here at this university. He'd understand."

"Understand what?"

They stared at each other for a moment before Frank turned his head away. "I'm sorry. This isn't like me. It's just I've been through one hell of an experience."

Graham took out a notebook. "Tell me about it."

Frank looked across the table and shrugged. "Why not? You won't believe me, but what have I got to lose?"

He settled into his chair, his hands clasped in front of him. "I'm not mad, nor am I suffering from psychotic delusions. I fully realize this is the year 1965 and the person who sits before you is eleven years old, in body at least. My mind is that of a fifty-eight-year-old nuclear physicist. You can't deny I use words and sentence structures no eleven-year-old would."

Graham held his features neutral. "Go on. I'm listening."

A second passed before Frank spoke again. "Just for a moment, pretend I'm sane. It's the year 2012 and I head a team in search of the Holy Grail of high energy plasma research, a controlled fusion reaction. Our grant money runs out in a week. We're desperate for results and worn out from long hours.

One morning, we start up another in a series of experiments. The lasers fire. The fuel pellets implode. There's a burst of energy, then a slow power build up as a miniature sun forms within the magnetic containment field. Everything's proceeding normally.

"At 10:45 an alarm sounds. Three gauges jump off the scale. I've made a serious error in a critical calculation. Within seconds the containment field will collapse, leading to a fiery explosion.

"Imagine yourself in that spot, Dr. Graham. You and all your of colleagues are going to die. There's nothing you can do to stop it. If you had one wish at that moment, what would it be? I'll tell you. You'd wish to go back one hour and fix that computer mistake. You'd wish it with all of your heart and all of your soul and all of your being.

"Now, imagine you make this wish. A high-pitched squeal tears though your head. The world squeezes into a single bright point. Your body is drawn out, elongated like a tube, and hurdles towards it. You might think the explosion came and you're either hallucinating or dead.

"But you'd be wrong, because all this happened to me. I reached that dot and passed through. The world expanded again. I sat in the control room, but the experiment hadn't begun. Everyone was still setting up.

I glanced at the clock. It read 9:45 A.M. One hour before the disaster."

Frank got up and paced around the room. "My hands shook as I poured a glass of water. When I checked the calculation in the computer, I found it was wrong by exactly the amount in my vision. But, that vision was so insane I convinced myself I subconsciously knew about the mistake and had just dozed off and dreamt about it.

"As we got closer to the start of the experiment, I found myself repeating conversations I'd just had. I knew what everyone would say. When the second repeated conversation happened, I wrote down every action I remembered and everything anyone said up to the point when the alarm bells went off. As I watched, people repeated each word in the exact order I noted.

"10:45 came. There were no alarms, no explosions. At 10:46 the strange sense of premonition ended."

Graham had heard many stories by many people. Some were mundane, some disjointed, others incoherent. He was no expert in physics and this young boy could simply have been well read. Still, there was a presence about him, the way he spoke, his mannerisms, which were unlike any eleven-year-old he had ever met.

Frank sat back down. "The incident wouldn't leave my mind. For months, I analyzed data from the experiment. Nothing made sense until one day, when I was about to doze off, it all fit together like a flash in my mind. I was dumbfounded. There, before me, was the face of time.

"It moves like a tide. We don't notice because we're riding with the wave. I can't imagine what drives it, but the accident somehow shifted my consciousness on it."

"You see, that's the only thing that can travel through time, consciousness, what you'd call the spirit or aura.

To transport anything physical through time would break the most fundamental law of physics, the conservation of matter and energy. Mass would have to be destroyed in one reality and created in another. That's simply not possible.

"Only my conscious essence moved to attach itself to the body it once inhabited. My first ride was uncontrolled, but the data showed how time jumps could be steered.

"I studied newspapers from the library archives for stock movements, political activity, business trends and technological advancements. Dates and companies and names were all committed to memory. Even now, I can recite them.

"Late one night, I entered the control room alone and set the values from the computer model as I did when I made the mistake. This time I altered the formula to only produce the time shift without an explosion. The power built up. I pictured myself in 1972 as I was about to enter college. The world squeezed into a dot and I was sucked though a straw-like tube. Everything expanded, and I was eighteen years old again.

"That autumn, I invested in all the right stocks, all the right bonds. I was a millionaire before summer. Two years later, I completed my undergraduate degree. In graduate school, I revealed knowledge of the scientific future in small, calculated packets. The world hailed me as a new Einstein."

Graham sat his pad down. "If everything worked out, why are you here?"

Frank stood up again and looked at the high window. "One day a racing bicycle passed me. I remembered how much I wanted one when I was fifteen but was afraid to ask my father for it. Then, I wished silently that I had asked. A simple wish. The world squeezed into a dot and I was fifteen years old.

"Somehow I was still floating free on the time tide. I panicked at first, then realized this was not really a disaster. The stock and bond prices were still fixed in my mind. I would just wait three years and start again.

"I guarded against every possible thought of the past and told myself to concentrate on the future. Then, a stray whim shunted me once more across the time tide to the age of fourteen. A few seconds later another thought pushed me here at the age of eleven. The shock was too much. I went into hysterics."

"There's something I don't understand, Frank. Why can't you just wish yourself to be eighteen again?"

"I've tried. It seems I can only go back."

Graham picked up his pad. "So, you believe somewhere in the future, there's a time machine that keeps interpreting random thoughts as requests?"

"No, that wouldn't happen. Everything was set to shut off one second after I left."

Frank clasped his hand across his mouth. "Oh God. How could I be so stupid? I left the time stream before the equipment shut down. The damned thing's out there in some possible future and it's still interpreting my wishes. Until I pass that point it will continue to run."

He got to his feet and paced the floor, "If only I could move forward in time, go to the start of the experiment and find a way to turn the machine off before I left."

Frank breathed in hard gasps. "I wish more than anything that I could go back to the beginning of it all."

A high-pitched screech ripped through the room. Graham clasped his hands over his ears. He looked up and let out a scream as he watched Frank's body squeeze into a long, thin tube and shoot toward a single, bright point.

Frank saw no light, heard no sound. His thoughts came in echoes that were slightly out of phase. One voice inside him called to another. That second voice moved with desperation to be reunited with the first.

No. Not reunited. Frank was being united for the first time. It was one second before his own conception. His mind was split between the egg and the sperm, the single combination of genetic material that would make the unique person called Frank.

The egg consciousness called. The sperm consciousness swam. As the two drew closer, Frank felt a sense of wholeness. It was truly a new beginning and this time there would be no mistakes.

His sperm consciousness gave a short mental laugh that slowed the movement of his vibrating tail just enough to allow another sperm to flash past and embed itself into the egg.

A nurse opened the door to examination room D. "Hello? Is anyone in here?"

Graham gave a start, as if awakened from a dream. He looked around with a sense of confusion. There was a table and two chairs, the nurse and himself, but no one else.

The nurse held the door open. "Doctor Graham? Is anything wrong?"

"Wrong?"

"The door was ajar and stopped to investigate."

Graham stared at the empty chair across the table, then at the blank page of his notebook. "Was I scheduled for a session in here today?"

"In here? You have a group therapy session in the executive conference room. Don't you remember?"

Graham stood slowly. "Yes. Of course. I'm so over extended I must've dosed off. When's the session start?"

"In fifteen minutes."

"Well, I don't know how I wound up here, but I better get going. Time and tide wait for no one."

SOMETHING ON MY MIND

CHAPTER ONE

*D*etective *Sgt. Chen. Meet me in my office.*
The silent summons came to my mind as though it were my own conscious thought.

There was always a slight hint of personality when one mind reached out to another across the world encompassing network known as The Connection through the links embedded in all our brains. The message came from my supervisor, Lieutenant Jenkins. I acknowledged the silent command and walked to the nearest Ramtube entrance to catch an InterCity to police headquarters.

The platform was deserted. It might have been that way for weeks. Few people found a need to leave the comfort of their apartments. They could use The Connection to reach anyone on Earth or have food, drink, clothes or whatever they desired produced and delivered by AI robots. They did everything. People no longer remembered how to provide for themselves. There was no need. The robots were efficient and infallible. I rarely went outside unless required to work on a case.

I wondered why Jenkins wanted to see me in person. Anything sensitive could be fed through a secure channel on The Connection.

An InterCity arrived, suspended and propelled by

linear magnets inside an evacuated tube. There was one other passenger, a young man who sat at the far end. Out of habit, I scanned his data in The Connection as police in past ages might have studied his face.

The other passenger was in closed mode, his thoughts private and unreachable. Still, as with every other human being on the planet, his carrier wave was connected to Central Control.

As a police officer, I was able to absorb his name, Frederick Shuller, along with a hundred other facts, in seconds. He had made some critical comments about the government in several forums, but they were not subversive. It wasn't a crime to think. The police were only concerned with those who acted out their thoughts.

The InterCity reached the Ruby Hansford Police Center, named after the legendary director who died in a selfless act a century before.

The lobby was deserted. I took an elevator to the illegal traffic division on the ninth floor. This had nothing to do with the ground vehicles of the past. Traffic was the movement of over through The Connection through our rain links.

My division tracked criminals who used illegal devices to alter links and adopt false identities or commandeer those of others in order to commit crimes. Tampering with The Connection was a felony with severe penalties.

Like every officer, Jenkins usually worked across the network unless he had to go out in the field. Still, every lieutenant and captain on the police force maintained a physical office. Jenkins motioned me inside. He silently transmitted, *"Close the door, George,"* through The Connection.

I sat down. *"Is there a reason we couldn't meet over a secure channel, sir?"*

"The captain wants us to try some in-person reviews to see if they gather more information. Just for the record. Detective Sergeant George Chen. Thirty-four years old. Single. Mother's name Mary. Ethnic Scandinavian. Father's name Yi. Ethnic Chinese. Residential region 4498645, address block 55699963 location 4489. Graduate of North Central Police Academy with honors. Promoted to sergeant two years ago."

I nodded.

We reviewed old cases I solved over the last few years. As Jenkins asked questions he certainly knew the answers to, I shifted in my seat and wondered just how long this would go on.

I was about to ask when Jenkins transmitted, *"You're doing a fine job, Detective Chen. That will be all."*

As I began to stand, Jenkins reached beneath his desk. Instantly, all the traffic in my head stopped. I could no longer sense the people in the other offices, on the street outside or in cities around the world. The vast databank libraries of facts, images and sounds were cut off. I experienced something I'd never known before—utter silence. It felt as though I'd been punched in the stomach.

I bit back a scream. My breath came in erratic spasms. I'd faced death several times as a police officer and was not ashamed to admit I knew fear. This was blind terror.

Thoughts formed, but remained locked in my head without the satisfying sensation that accompanies the acknowledgment of a receipt signal. I leaped to my feet, drew my tranquer pistol from my jacket pocket and searched for an assailant.

Jenkins spoke aloud in a calming voice. "It's all right, George. Please, sit down."

I returned to my chair. "Is The Connection down?" Even as I spoke the words, I knew that wasn't possible. In its entire existence, The Connection had never failed. There were too many redundancies.

My voice was hoarse from more than apprehension. I was out of practice. A person had little need for speech after the age of four when a link is installed in the brain.

Jenkins said, "I cut the traffic. I had to. No one can know what I'm about to tell you, even on a secure channel."

The lieutenant poured some water into a glass and pushed it across the desk. "I know. It's quite a shock."

I grabbed the glass with both hands and took a sip. A stinging sense filled me as if I were a cowering child instead of a seasoned police detective. "You could have warned me."

Jenkins shook his head. "I couldn't. No one can know we're even having this conversation. That's why the pretense of a review at the beginning."

He smiled. "If it's any consolation, I nearly wet myself the first time I lost The Connection. I still don't like it, but sometimes Captain Barnes has to tell me things no one else can learn about. This time I have to tell you. That's why I've blocked all traffic within these walls. Even our carrier waves have been cut off."

The most fundamental rule of The Connection was a carrier wave couldn't be blocked. The devices implanted into every brain constantly transmitted a person's condition to Central Control.

"That's impossible," I said.

"There are ways, but it requires the authorization of a

director. That should give you some idea of how high up this goes. You can imagine the alarms in Central Control right now if I hadn't been given that authorization. Two days ago, they did go off. On Tuesday, the carrier wave of a forty-seven-year-old male named Phillip Santos disappeared from Central Control's sensors."

"Disappeared?" This was unbelievable. The self-powered unit in Santos' brain would continue to broadcast his carrier wave even if he died.

Jenkins clasped his hands behind his head. "That's the mystery. It wasn't a hijacking or redirection. Santos just vanished. Somehow, he unlinked himself."

"Why would he do such a thing?" I tried to imagine life without my link. It would be impossible to enter an apartment or order food. A person might just as well stop breathing.

Jenkins leaned forward. "That's what we want you to find out, George. Only a handful of people know about Santos. It's the reason we had to meet outside the network. If word of this gets out, there'll be panic. Who knows where Santos is and what he plans to do. The captain isn't sure if this is an isolated incident or part of a wider conspiracy."

Instinctually, I called on The Connection for facts, figures, and opinions as I normally would. Nothing came. Without these lifelong aids, I had to concentrate intently to make sense of what Jenkins was saying.

The lieutenant said, "You took a pseudo tour in the area around the Grand Canyon in North America last year, didn't you?"

I nodded. The summer before, I'd lain on my bed while a medibot inserted feeder tubes into my arms to sustain me. Then, I jumped across The Connection to implant my consciousness into the mind of a local resident, a host who rented out his body for people to hike, explore, and soak up the warm sun as if they were actually there.

It wasn't just an impression. I lost all conscious awareness of my own body as my mind was coupled to my host's senses; sight, sound, touch, taste and smell. I had complete control over every muscle of the host. It was a wonderful week and I came back refreshed without ever physically leaving my home.

Jenkins said, "Santos last accessed The Connection to pay for a meal at a retro-resort in the desert region just south of the canyon."

Retro-resorts ranged in size from small spas to entire towns. They recreated articular periods in history with costumes, food, entertainment and speech. People who wanted to feel as if they'd stepped back in time traveled physically to a resort and took on the persona of someone from that era. I heard about the resort on my pseudo tour. The whole town was set in the mid-twentieth century.

Jenkins said, "He stayed in a motel named The Wooden Spoke."

"Motel?"

"A type of lodging for travelers. They were popular when people still used ground transportation. He was in room six. A judge issued a search warrant for the entire motel. There's an air car in the garage with all the necessary maps loaded. We also packed a case with clothes and incidentals. You leave immediately."

"How often should I report?"

"You don't, not until you find Santos. Between now and then no one can know where you are or what you find."

He brought out a round, flat object just larger than a thumb. "This is a Cdisk. They were once used as currency. It's powered by the heat of people's fingers and filled with a small fortune to cover your expenses."

Jenkins took a rectangular object out of a desk drawer. It was a thin, plastic sheet a little larger than his hand. He unfolded it to four times that size.

I recognized it, but had never seen one before. They were the primary method of conveying and analyzing information before The Connection. Its official name was Thin Membrane Data Appliance. People referred to them as thims.

Jenkins said, "This contains all the data you'll need for the assignment. It was synchronized with The Connection just before you came in. I've unlinked it to prevent anyone from tracking you. It'll be invaluable for research, but it has another important function. When you find Santos, press these three symbols simultaneously. The thim will re-link with The Connection and send a homing signal to Central Control.

"I could just use a secure channel."

"You won't be able to."

The door to Jenkins's office opened. A tall, humanoid robot entered. Even though the robot had no need for clothes, it still wore a white coat.

Jenkins said, "I'm sorry, George. No one can know where you are. The medibot is here to unlink you."

CHAPTER TWO

As the self-driving aircar sped toward the retro-resort, I studied reports about Phillip Santos on the thim. Few people knew how to read. I learned in my first year at the academy. Police officers often discover records from the time before Central Control or evidence written in the ancient form by criminals.

I fumbled with the representation of symbols displayed on the plastic surface of the thim. Every entry or query was cumbersome and took far too much time. If I'd still been linked, the information would have come in an instant.

The sky was nearly empty. That was no surprise. Few people wasted time to travel anywhere physically when they could reach out to the world with a thought, see any place, smell the aromas, hear the sounds, taste the delicacies, touch the fabric of the world all through The Connection. The only other aircars I encountered in the sky were robot craft in transit to maintain the vast technological infrastructure.

I had no idea how this was done. No one did. It had been generations since a human was required to repair anything. The robots were quick and efficient. They even built and repaired themselves. Robots of various shapes and sizes prepared the food everyone ate, designed the clothes they wore, and produced the entertainment. I was nearly addicted to an AI generated *cerbdrama* I absorbed into my mind every Tuesday night about a family and its financial empire. This week's episode would clear up the paternity of the president's oldest son.

Audiences were immersed into the shows as though they were characters themselves. If I didn't find Santos in a few days, I'd miss the next chapter. I could wait to experience it in archive, but that would take a month and I would lose the story line by then.

The Wooden Spoke was a one story, stucco building in the shape of the letter L. It sprawled across the desert at the edge of the resort.

Near the road was an office. Along the rest of the building were pairs of doors and windows. Metal boxes with grills protruded through the walls, one set below each window. The thim identified them as air conditioners for cooling the rooms. My apartment kept itself at a constant, comfortable temperature.

I stepped out of the air car and was slammed by a wall of hot, dry air. I wiped sweat from my forehead and hoped the air conditioners worked.

There were three other aircars in the parking lot. To my surprise, a wheeled vehicle came down the road and passed in front of the motel. I'd never seen anything like it before. It was smaller than an aircar and shaped like an oblong box with two wheels on each side that rolled along the ground and an open cockpit. There were two padded benches, one in front of the other, and a transparent visor positioned directly in front of the cockpit. One person sat on the front bench and another on the rear. They waved as they sped by with a roaring whoosh. I smiled and waved back.

As I walked into the office, a bell tinkled. A clerk behind a desk stood as I approached. He must have assumed I was in closed mode and spoke with a slight twang in his voice. "Yes sir, can I help you?"

The air conditioner blew a steady stream of cold air into the room. It was both chill and refreshing at the same instant. I stepped up to the desk. "I'd like a room."

The man slid a book and pen across the counter. "I think we can accommodate you. We don't get many guests in the high summer." He opened the registration book. "Sign here, please."

I signed in and examined the book. "Is this actual paper?"

"One-hundred percent genuine. We like to give that complete experience of the past Mr.…" The clerk looked down at the ledger, "Chen. It's always nice to meet a gentleman who knows how to write. You can probably guess I like to keep the old traditions alive. How long are you staying?"

"A few nights. I'm expecting a friend."

"Always glad to hear that. How would you like to pay?"

Normally, I would use The Connection to open a conduit to my credit account and pass it to the clerk. Instead, I laid the Cdisk on the desk. "I hope you take this."

The clerk smiled. "Of course we do. No one's used one of these all season. You're obviously a man who likes to play the game." He placed the disk over a circle. It flashed red, then changed to steady green.

The clerk handed the disk back, along with a metal

key. "Do you know how to use one of these?"

"Yes, thank you. As I said, I'm waiting for a friend."

I displayed Santos' image on the thim.

The man's eyes opened wide as he gazed at the device. "I've only heard about these things, but I've never seen one before. You've got all the toys."

He studied the picture. "Sure. I remember him. Paul Bass, right? I'm afraid he beat you here. Came in a couple of days ago."

I noted the assumed name. "That's Paul all right. Did he use his Cdisk?"

"No. Paid over The Connection. Funny. Now that I think about it, I haven't seen him for a couple of days."

"Did he mention anything about where he was going or what he wanted to do?"

"Not a thing. His aircar's still out in the lot. The blue Starcruiser. He may have taken a hover bus out to the Painted Desert or up to the canyon. I'll let him know you're here."

"Do me a favor. Don't mention me. I want to give him a surprise."

"Sure thing. Enjoy your stay."

CHAPTER THREE

I put my case in the room and walked into town. The buildings spanned a period from the nineteenth to the mid-twentieth century. Signs read bank, pharmacy and souvenirs. One building had canisters in front of it and a sign that read Gas. The ground vehicle I saw at the motel was parked next to one of the cylinders with a hose that connected the two.

What surprised me most was the number of people gathered together in one place. They stood on corners and walked along sidewalks, sat together on benches and visited the shops. There were dozens of them, and they all talked aloud to each other.

On one corner of the main street stood a two-story building with a sign labeled Rattlesnake Cafe. I took a seat on a counter stool inside. The air was a clash of exotic aromas, some sharp, some subtle, and others thick. A buzz of conversation echoed off the varnished pine walls. For an instant, the jumble of voices reminded me of the background hum of The Connection.

A woman with an apron tied around her waist wiped the counter in front of me with a damp towel. Like the motel clerk, she spoke with a twang in her voice. "What'll ya' have?"

I looked at the menu. "What's good?"

"New in town, hey? Try the fried chicken basket. You'll like it." She smiled and gave a wink.

I smiled back. "All right. Sounds good."

She wrote the order on a small pad of paper, ripped it out of the book and stuck it on a horizontal, metal wheel set between the serving area and the kitchen where I spied humanoid robots who prepared meals.

Food always meant things like crisp grain wafers, soft puddings with subtle flavors, clear broth in the summer and hearty soups in autumn, all prepared in factories by robots and delivered to my apartment.

The robots knew what to bring. I never thought about it. Every meal was nutritionally balanced, flavor neutral and consistently the same. No one knew how the robots produced them. I'd never actually seen a vegetable, or a slice of fruit, and certainly not a piece of cooked animal flesh.

I stared down at a plastic basket lined with red and white checkered paper. A deep-fried chicken leg, chicken breast and strips of fried potatoes sat upon it, I felt nauseous.

I looked up at the waitress. She seemed to sense my distress. Her voice dropped out of the slight twang she'd affected and became monotone. "Would you like to change your order, sir?"

I swallowed hard. "No. If I paid for it I'd better eat it, right?"

The waitress nodded and adopted the resort speech again. "Ya'. Sure. Would you like anything else?"

"I'm just waiting for a friend. He seems to have

wandered off." I brought out the thim and showed her Santos' picture. "You haven't seen him, have you?"

She looked at it for a second. "Paul Bass, right? Haven't seen him today." She moved off to serve another customer.

I looked at the chicken leg and brought it to my mouth. There was a strange aroma I couldn't identify. It didn't smell appetizing.

With a bite, the crunchy coating reminded me of crackers and tasted quite good. The consistency of the meat was like nothing I'd ever eaten. The taste was not unpleasant, yet at the same time, it was not inspiring. I liked the potato strips, however. The combination of crispy and soft was unique. I would certainly try them again.

I got up and went to the cash register. The thim informed me a custom from this period was to leave a payment in addition to the bill for the server. I left a healthy amount.

Over the next few hours, I visited every shop, repeated my story and showed the image. Several people met Santos a few days before. None of them knew where he might be. Santos used the name Bass everywhere in town.

This was a puzzle. If Santos was connected, his real identity would be instantly fed to anyone he opened up to when he paid his bill. Criminals with illegal devices could broadcast false identities for a short time, long enough to make a single financial transaction or commit an assault. No one could possibly generate a false identity more than once a day. The strain was just too intense. Santos used the identity of Paul Bass continuously since he arrived.

I returned to the motel and consulted the thim for references to monetary transactions and aircar rentals over the last two years in the name Paul Bass.

One account caught my eye. It showed months of inactivity when there was only a carrier wave followed by a few weeks of credits for visits to the resort, followed by several more months of inactivity and then more visits.

The last transaction was for a meal at the Rattlesnake Cafe three days before. I was certain I'd found the suspect, but who was he? Could Phillip Santos be the pseudonym and Paul Bass the real person? If Jenkins could block the carrier wave, could someone else create a false one?

When it got dark, I took the thim out to the parking lot. There were some decorative lights along the front of the motel and down the covered walkway by the rooms. The parking area was in shadow.

Above my head was a multitude of stars. They were rarely visible outside my window against the constant glare of city lights at night. I stood in the dark and gazed at the deep black background and brilliant white points above me. Anyone could connect to one of the astronomical telescopes and explore the galaxy through their lenses, of course. Still, the sheer expanse of the night sky took my breath away. It was as if a veil was torn from my eyes.

I reached Santos' Starcruiser and held the thim in front of it. The security system had not been set. There were no identity tags and the thim revealed the aircar had no sensor link. It was electronically invisible to any guidance system. Santos must have flown the machine manually the entire way. That would be exhausting, a feat I wouldn't relish.

I commanded the thim to unlock the door, then checked beneath the carpet on the floor and felt along the lining of the roof. The thim opened the rear engine compartment so I could examine everything inside. I checked the luggage area. There were no clues to be found.

I went to Santos' room. The thim found one standard security alarm and disconnected it. I used a skill I'd learned as a cadet— but never imagined I'd need— to mechanically pick the lock.

I slipped on a pair of low-light lenses and began a search with a scan from the thim for any movement patterns on the carpet. Someone paced in front of the bed, walked to the window several times and to the desk once.

I checked dresser drawers, under the bed and on top of the desk. As in my room, the desk held a lamp, a blotter and an ancient communication device the thim identified as a telephone.

In the bathroom, I lifted the lid of the antique toilet tank, scanned behind mirrors and checked for loose tiles. Back in the room, I reached between the mattress and box springs. My hand touched a small metal canister. Inside was a slip of paper with an address, 356 Chelsea St. Glendale. There was a message beneath the address, "Aunt Ruby sent me. I've got something on my mind and she said you could help." Within seconds, the paper turned black and crumbled in my hand.

I pulled out one of the drawers and examined the bottom. It had the number 5268 written on it in ink. I assumed the marks were centuries old and started to put the drawer back in place when a thought came to me. The thim reported each telephone had a unique local number made up of seven digits. The first three were an exchange within a service area.

In my own room, I located a telephone directory. It was only three pages long. Every number started with

357. There was no entry for 3575268.

It was nearly midnight when I went to bed. Without the familiar background of network traffic in my mind, it was hard to fall asleep.

Just before dawn, I awoke and instinctively tried to get a news report from The Connection, then remembered I couldn't.

I read the instructions on a device in the room that was supposed to make a drink called coffee. The thim reported coffee was once a popular beverage used by people to wake themselves up.

The smell was pleasant. I took a sip and grimaced at the bitter taste. "They can keep that part of their twentieth century." I stopped and, with some sense of amusement, realized I'd spoken aloud to myself.

The sun streamed into the room, the sign of another hot day. I tapped instructions into the thim, placed the telephone on top of it, picked up the receiver and dialed 3575268.

There was a sound like a bell, then a click.

A man's voice said, "Hello?"

"Hello. Is Larry Bass there?"

"I'm sorry. You have a wrong number."

There was another click and the line blared a dissident toner.

I lifted the telephone and removed the thim, which had recorded the minute delay of my voice as it echoed through the handset at the other end and back again. The second telephone was somewhere just outside the resort.

To bolster my cover as a retro-tourist, I boarded a hover bus with ten other people for a trip to the south rim of the Grand Canyon.

On my pseudo tour the year before, I'd used my host's body to hike around the rim and down into the canyon as far as the Colorado River and an overnight hostel. The sights, the sounds, the smells were all familiar, yet there was something different this time. As I stood there in person and took in the vista with my own eyes, it seemed oddly less real. At the same time, it was more present. There was an unseen weight to this huge gash in the Earth that pressed on my shoulders.

I returned to town that afternoon and visited the local telephone exchange to trace the switches and discover where the mystery number was located. The equipment proved too unsophisticated for the thim to scan.

I asked the woman in the exchange about telephones. "How far do the wires run?"

"Just inside the resort."

"No one has a telephone out in the desert?"

"Oh no. They're just for show. Outside of the resort you'd use The Connection."

I made more enquiries around town about the history of the retro-resort and if anyone still lived in the desert but learned nothing of any use.

After dinner, a magnificent sunset lit the desert sky in intense shades of reds and yellows. The colors faded into pastels as the sun dropped over the horizon.

It was a warm evening and I walked around town for a while. The oppressive heat of the day subsided and more people congregated on the streets and corners. They smiled and talked and laughed.

My mind worked on the case as I walked along. I turned a corner and found myself alone in a dark alley with neither doors nor windows. The sound of a metallic bang echoed between the buildings. I drew my tranquer pistol.

A hollow, metal barrel rocked back and forth on its side in a little depression in the pavement. I used my foot to stop it and found the barrel quite heavy.

From the edge of my peripheral vision, I caught a glimpse of a shape. It disappeared into the street. The mystery shadow might have only been a dog, but it would have to have been a very large one to knock over a barrel like that.

I made my way back to the motel. In the morning, I would take Santos' aircar to explore the desert area.

The room was still hot. The press of a button on the air conditioner sent cool air over my body. I left the Cdisk in a pocket of my pants and placed the thim and tranquer on a small table next to the bed within easy reach.

In the bathroom, I splashed water on my face.

A sickeningly sweet smell wafted through the room. My arms grew heavy. My head became light. The world turned black.

CHAPTER FOUR

I awoke in a narrow bed jammed against the wall of a windowless room. My head ached. The tranquer and thim were nowhere to be seen.

It seemed like hours passed before the only door opened and two men entered.

One carried an old-style projectile pistol.

The other said, "Follow us."

We walked down a hallway to a room with a glass, picture window. It overlooked a desert canyon. Cacti and low brush covered the ground. Sharp, craggy hills loomed in the near distance, their sides striated in hues of tan, brown and red.

Someone sat in a high-backed chair turned away to face the window. Thin elbows jutted out to each side.

The guards loosened their grips and stepped back one pace.

The person in the chair spoke with the voice of an older woman. "So many misconceptions about the desert, Mr. Chen. People rarely come here now. It's thought of as a wasteland, dead and useless. Look for yourself. There are dozens of species, plant and animal, out on that floor. Some live only here. They are at the edge of existence.

Every year more deserts vanish as they're paved over and plugged into The Connection. What do you think happened to all of those plants and animals that used to live there?"

I weighed my response and decided to remain neutral. "I don't know."

With a smooth swivel, the chair turned to reveal a woman in her eighties. Her white hair was cropped short. She was thin to the point of being gaunt. "They all died. There was nowhere for them to go. The jack rabbits and tortoises and lizards and snakes and coyotes. All dead. Plants and animals can't get out of the way of a society intent on running them over, but people can, with some help."

I knew of groups investigated for their demands to return lands to their wild states. None of them broke traffic laws, so I'd never encountered them. In fact, they used The Connection to further their causes. It made no sense one of them would be involved with anyone who unlinked himself.

The guard with the gun motioned toward a couch.

I sat down.

The woman pointed to the men. "This is Franz with the pistol and Hans standing behind you. Everyone here calls me Aunt Ruby. Gentlemen, this is George Chen, our latest guest and something of a puzzle."

I looked to Franz and Hans and formed what I hoped was a pleasant smile. "I'm glad to meet you, though I'm a little disoriented. Do you know the way back to the resort?"

Aunt Ruby studied me. "So many questions, Mr. Chen. That's part of the puzzle. You ask questions of almost everyone at the resort. Then you call here and ask the wrong question."

Aunt Ruby motioned to Hans.

He pulled my head forward. I felt him slide open the cover over my link.

Aunt Ruby inspected it, then stepped back. "There are no lights. You're not transmitting a carrier wave. That's a serious crime. Aren't you afraid of prison?"

"What would you know of prison?"

"I know much of how the world works. My name is Ruby Hansford. Director Ruby Hansford."

I cleared my throat. "I guess we're playing a little game. You're pretending to be a director who gave her life over a century ago to save a city. Who should I play? Seriously, who are you?"

"It's not my identity that's in question here, Mr. Chen. You arrive with a broken link and without any of the usual messages from the field. You make inquiries about Paul Bass, a very particular name, even call this telephone and ask for him. Forgive my bluntness, but that seems just a little suspicious."

"Well, yes. I am unlinked. I don't know what happened. I've been avoiding the authorities. The person who broke my link said I'd find a telephone number written under a drawer."

Aunt Ruby sat in the chair. "What is the name of that person?"

I fought not to squirm. "He didn't say. I couldn't see him. I was blindfolded and taken somewhere by aircar."

Hans said, "Where to?"

There was no way to tell how far this operation spread. I hoped it was in large cities. "Tokyo."

Hans turned to Aunt Ruby.

She nodded, then leaned forward. "Why did you want to unlink from The Connection?"

This was a question I was unprepared for. Nothing in the investigation indicated a motive for Santos to break his link. I decided to be noncommittal. "That's rather personal."

Franz kept the gun trained on me. "No one is completely unlinked in the field. It makes the journey here too difficult and dangerous."

Aunt Ruby stood and walked over to me. "Several people who knew they were dying allowed their carrier waves to be extracted and stored in devices. Clients have their links overridden with those carrier waves when they're disconnected in the field. Each person is provided with a unique password."

"We were interrupted by the police before the carrier wave could be transferred. There was no time to learn a password."

Aunt Ruby shook her head. "When I first learned about your arrival, I hoped you were indeed a client who'd lost his way, but your story is just too improbable. It's evident you're someone else, a police officer from the Illegal Traffic Division sent to investigate the disconnection of Phillip Santos. We've been expecting someone."

Hans said, "The truth is you're not here to investigate Phillip Santos. You were sent to flush out the lioness. You've found her."

Whoever these people were, they were organized beyond anything I or the police force were aware of. I stared at the woman as I took in Franz's position and calculated how to wrestle the gun from him.

As if Hans read my mind, he clamped his hands on

my shoulder.

Aunt Ruby looked into my eyes. "I am indeed former director Ruby Hansford, and quite alive. It was less than fifty years ago when I was one of the directors, an administrator of the planet. The other directors changed the historical records in The Connection and made it seem I vanished a century ago to fit their lies."

I shook my head. "That's impossible. No one can alter data in The Connection. It's the standard of truth."

Aunt Ruby sat back down. "When I was a director, I discovered a threat to our world so great it will one day lead to the extinction of the human race. I expected a swift response when I reported it, but not the one I received. I was accused of spreading subversive lies and declared a traitor. A secret security force unknown even to the police seized me. My link was broken so my thoughts couldn't contaminate anyone else."

"There is no secret security force. Everything the directors do is open for all to examine."

Franz said, "We were once lied to the same as you."

Aunt Ruby paused a moment, as if in contemplation. "The three primary directors hold many deep and dark secrets, Mr. Chen. Some even I was unaware of.

"They banished me to a place beneath the Earth where I cleared sludge and soil from sewers with my bare hands. Beside me worked men and women who expressed ideas considered subversive. They were hunted down by the security forces.

"I'm not certain how long we labored in the wretched muck until I found a way to escape through forgotten service tunnels and took a group of prisoners with me. Without links, Central Control couldn't track us. We lived in those tunnels for years, raided other prison camps and even surface stores to provide for our needs. Inside the abandoned tunnels I discovered forgotten conduits where we could tap into The Connection with devices we stole."

Hans said, "I was one of those who escaped with Aunt Ruby. Ever since, we've listened to the traffic. We reveal neither our location nor our thoughts. Central Control knows about our taps. They send robots to destroy them and we set up new ones. Through the taps we learned of the assignment to find Phillip Santos, though we didn't know who would come or when."

I now understood the real reason Lieutenant Jenkins was ordered to shield our conversation from The Connection, and why my link was broken. It was obvious I had no chance of denying who I was. I slipped and allowed my voice to show sarcasm. "And what is this great disaster?"

A look of sympathy came to Aunt Ruby's eyes. "This must be difficult for you. All you've ever know is The Connection. I understand. Once, I thought as you do."

I tried to determine exactly what her game was. There seemed to be no financial incentive. They certainly had enough zeal to be anarchists. The house might be packed with explosives. It was impossible to tell if this woman was the leader or if this was just a cell. The only thing I could do was to keep my head and wait for an opportunity.

Hans said, "We should show him."

Aunt Ruby nodded. "Bring him to the work room."

Franz motioned for me to rise and follow Aunt Ruby.

Hans fell in line behind.

We walked down a hallway. Aunt Ruby said, "As a director I was devoted to Central Control and The Connection. After being banished to those pits, I discovered the truth about what we've become."

I said, "You can't destroy The Connection. It holds society together."

Aunt Ruby stopped and turned to me. "We don't intend to destroy anything. The problem isn't with The Connection. It's with us and how we use it. When was the last time you talked to a friend about your dreams?"

"No one has to talk. You just link to someone and everything is transferred."

"Everything?"

"Everything you want them to know. That's what closed mode is for. People want to share their thoughts, not have their minds read."

She half smiled. "Yes. There are things we want to keep private—unpleasant thoughts we may have about our boss, tender feelings for someone who we fear will not return them. We learn at an early age to guard our thoughts and repress strong emotions. Parents and teachers discipline children if they let too much out. All communication is bland and superficial. No one shares their true feelings less a thought brand them a dissident in the eyes of Central Control."

Hans said, "At one time there were many connections. To reduce costs, several local directors merged theirs with others. There were protests, especially from societies who feared becoming absorbed into the larger ones and losing their unique identity, culture and language. Assurances were given, but the homogenization took place in the name of efficiency. Many customs and languages were supplanted with those of the larger partner. Merger after merger took place until there was one connection and one authority, Central Control."

We entered a large room. A table sat in the middle. Shelves lined the walls. With a start, I realized they were bound paper books. I'd never seen so many in one place before. What few existed were in museum archives.

Several non-humanoid robots were arranged in a corner. They were in various states of disassembly. Parts of robots lay next to them.

Aunt Ruby took a book from a shelf. She indicated one of the robots.

Hans retrieved it and sat it on the table. "This is a Type 48R food service robot."

Aunt Ruby pointed to the book. "These are the technical specifications for it. The circuit to open doors is broken. Everything you need to know to make a repair is in this drawing. We've read the dossier of every officer in your division through our taps. Yours says you have training in electronics, even built a racing robot. What would you do?"

I studied the page set out before me and examined the robot. From my hobby with electronics, it was evident the drawing was a schematic. I even knew what some of the symbols meant. This robot was far more complex than the one I built as a youth. I thought I could make out a power supply, but wasn't certain. It seemed a random mess of wires and circuit boards. "I can't repair robots. I don't have to. They build and maintain themselves."

Aunt Ruby said, "That's how it was intended to work. The instructions have become corrupted over time in the central depositories and spread to each robot's internal mechanism, like a cancer. It's a code stored on physical media designed to last for centuries and sent through a separate network created for machine efficiency independent of the Connection. The media is decaying. No one knows how to retrieve the initial data or flush the system and reestablish the correct instructions."

Franz said, "Robots are breaking down around the world. The failure rate for replacement robots is over 80%. Human prisoners now cannibalize broken robots to maintain others."

This was the most preposterous story yet. "If that's true, the directors would have fixed the problems already. All knowledge is available to everyone."

Aunt Ruby pointed to the book. "Yes. It's before your eyes right here, yet you can't use the information because the underlying science and technology has been lost. These technical manuals are available to the directors. No one can interpret them."

I looked at the robot again. "Nonsense. The directors could find someone to figure it out. People can think."

"Yes, said Hans. "Human beings can learn and act, yet all knowledge of science and technology was turned over to AI robots generations ago. No human is capable of either repairing them or doing the work they perform. When the code is corrupted to a level where no more robots can be built or repaired, there will be no one to provide medical care, maintain infrastructure or even grow food. This is what will lead to our extinction as a species."

Aunt Ruby put the book back on the shelf. "Now, the last of the artists and scientists are gone. Most of the old records outside The Connection were destroyed. Even data in The Connection has been compromised to suit the ambitions of the directors. Members of our group search the world for sites with lost and hidden knowledge to relearn the forgotten skills needed to survive before it's too late. We call those locations honey flowers and those who seek them honeybees."

Franz said, "It took time for the directors to seize power. It didn't have to be that way, but people allowed it for the promise of comfort and convenience."

Aunt Ruby looked up to the ceiling. "I remember being a very small child when my great grandfather told of how things were before The Connection—a world with war, crime, poverty, hunger and injustice. He spoke of his generation's vision of grand nobility where all would be equal and secure without want or need with every desire just a thought away. Humanity would be freed from the drudgery of everyday toil to think and create. They envisioned those thoughts excelling to create new and wondrous things in a utopia."

She turned her gaze back to me. "That was the dream, repeated over and over. Instead, The Connection became a trap. The machines provide everything and everyone is bound and dependent on them. People have lost the ability to think or create or adapt. The expression of thoughts, feelings and ideas people were afraid to think for themselves were turned over to the robots. No one could blame a machine for an idea. At one time, all music, art, storytelling and humor was created by people as their expression of humanity. Now, these things are produced exclusively by AI robots who provide the illusion of culture without the risk someone might displease Central Control."

Hans put the robot back on the floor. "There was a problem with the link provided to Mr. Santos. It transmitted the pseudo identity of Paul Bass, but continued to broadcast Santos' own carrier wave. We discovered this too late to keep Central Control from tracing the signal to the retro-resort."

Aunt Ruby turned to me with a sad look on her face. "We'll have to shut down this operation, but we have others. The directors know everything I've told you, though they still deny the truth. I don't know if I've convinced you. Still, I'm glad we were able to have this little chat."

Hans grabbed me from behind. I felt a stab in my arm. The room seemed to spin before I lost consciousness.

CHAPTER FIVE

When I woke in my motel room it was nearly sundown. I activated the thim and pressed the three symbols Lt. Jenkins showed me in his office.

In moments, unmarked aircars touched down in the parking lot. I ran out of the room and waved my arms. "Over here. I found…"

An officer pulled out her tranquer pistol and squeezed the trigger.

I froze in place as every voluntary muscle in my body seized up. A tranq hit isn't painful. Your heart and breath remain normal. You can still think clearly. You just can't move except to blink your eyes.

I was lifted into one of the aircars. A hood was placed over my head as the whir of the machine increased. No one spoke. A tranq usually wears off in fifteen minutes. I remained immobilized long past that.

The car landed. Hands placed me on a stretcher, though I still couldn't see through the hood. The whoosh of several doors opened and closed before the stretcher stopped and I was lifted into a chair. Straps secured my legs and chest. With the prick of a needle, control returned to my muscles. The hood was removed and I opened my eyes.

I sat in a hard, straight-backed chair. Bright lights shone in my face. I looked up to a large, semi-circular desk where thirteen men and women sat. They wore white robes with long sleeves. All had shaved heads.

A man in the center stood. "Welcome, Detective Chen. We are the directors. I am Director Penton."

There was a flutter in my chest. No one ever saw the directors. These were the people who controlled the world and everything in it. I, George Chen, was in the presence of the most powerful of the powerful. My breath quickened.

Director Peton raised a hand. "Please, detective. Don't be nervous."

I tried to compose myself. "It's just I never dreamed I would meet you. I'm deeply honored."

A woman stood."It is we who are honored. I am Director Weston. You have risked your life to combat a disease that would destroy our world. These rebels hate us and all we love. Their goal is nothing short of world destruction. They can't be appeased, only hunted down."

I began to describe the case when the woman stopped me. "There's no need to give a report. Your investigation is commendable, but we were not interested in Phillip Santos. We planned for you to be abducted by the criminals."

A numb tingle ran down my fingers. "But, I met them. I can identify their leader, a woman who told this ridiculous tale about the robots degrading. We have to go back and find that house. They're there right now. Hook me back into The Connection and you'll know who the leader is."

Director Weston said, "We already know. We knew before you left. We don't have to hook you back in. In fact, we can't."

A nagging panic worked its way up my back and into my throat. "Is there a malfunction?"

Director Penton pursed his lips. "Our society survives with the certainty all thought, all ideas, are open and free. Everyone must believe this. When certainty wavers, people become worried. Productivity falls. Unhappiness rises. Are you happy, detective Chen?"

"Of course."

Director Weston tilted her head. "Yet, a seed was planted in you. A question you may reject now, but it will never leave you. Imagine if you told Lieutenant Jenkins about your case. He would carry your question, however subtle, in the back of his mind. If he were to share the case with his supervisors, the question would grow. With enough mass, too many people would have the question and some would believe it."

My eyes took in the directors in a sweep. "I'm not spreading rumors. Anyone who looks into my mind will know I believe this woman's claims are a lie. I don't know what she thinks she can gain by making the story up."

Another director said, "She didn't make it up. The AI robots are breaking down and no one knows how to stop it yet. The most advanced engineering robots are working on the problem and we are confident there is a solution. In the meantime, we will continue to use broken robots to keep the others running."

I shook my head. "It can't be true. This woman is a pathological liar. She expected me to believe she was Director Hansford."

Director Weston said, "She didn't lie. You did meet Director Ruby Hansford. She only disappeared 50 years ago. We altered history in The Connection to make it seem she died a century before."

Director Penton looked at me as if I were an ignorant child. "If any of this became public knowledge there would be panic, riots, deaths. Ignorance can be an important tool for leaders When uninformed people are told they're happy, they will be happy."

Bile rose from my stomach to burn the back of my throat. "You changed The Connection? How can anyone do that? It's the ultimate storehouse of truth. When the AI robots fail everyone will starve. No one has the knowledge to produce food. You have to teach people how to do that now and not rely on fixing the robots before it's too late. You're supposed to protect us. I thought Aunt Ruby was a traitor. It's clear to me now. She and her team are trying to regain that knowledge before it's too late. You have to work with her, not persecute her. If you don't, you're the traitors."

Director Weston folded her arms over her chest. "You see, Detective Chen. Another doubt arises in you. This is why we can't allow you to rejoin. It will be reported you died in the line of duty. There will be a lavish funeral."

"You intend to kill me?"

"We don't commit murder. That's immoral. There are other services citizens can provide that do not require a link to The Connection."

Director Penton formed a placid smile. " We're sorry, detective. You served with distinction and honor."

Two men entered the room and undid the straps. They dragged me down a corridor and into an elevator.

I fought and struggled to break free to no avail. "Let me go. I'm a police detective."

The taller man slapped me. "We don't care who

you were. The directors declared you a traitor and that's all we need to know."

The elevator descended for a long time. We exited to a small alcove with a wire fence gate.

An immense cavern extended up several stories and out beyond visible sight.

One of the men took a small box from his pocket and pressed the button on it. The gate opened and they pulled me through.

A white-haired man in tattered clothes stood outside a small shack.

The taller man said, "Mr. Green, this is George Chen. He's been convicted of treason but wants to contribute to society. Do you have work for him?"

The other man handed Mr. Green an envelope.

Green opened it and studied the paper inside. "Yes. He may contribute to society. Please leave him with me."

I watched the two men leave, then turned to Green. "There's some mistake. I'm a police detective, not a traitor. I was on a serious case to hunt down traitors. Tap into The Connection and you'll know who I am."

Green studied me before speaking. "There is no link here. You've been entombed to serve the directors. You'll receive two meals a day and be expected to work while you're awake. Slackers and malcontents are not tolerated. The directors won't sully their hands with executions. I will. Follow me."

We moved through tunnels and caverns that resembled the ones Aunt Ruby described. People cleared sewage with their hands in U shaped troughs that led to large pipes where others worked. They toiled nonstop. No one looked at anyone else. Some fell where they toiled and laid motionless. People with whips urged them to get up. Those that didn't move were collected by hand carts and hauled away.

I'd never seen anything like this. There was no starvation in the world above. Violence was committed by criminals and the authorities arrested them. Here, violence was the tool of authority. All the concepts I held for morality made the scene nearly impossible to believe.

A whip cracked over the back of a man who panted on his hands and knees. I recognized him as Fredrick Shuller, who I saw in the Intercity on my way to police headquarters. I pointed. "I know him. He only expressed some critical ideas but never committed a crime."

The guard snapped the whip again.

Shuller began to move sludge with his hands.

Green pushed me forward. "You'll get used to it."

He escorted me to a metal door set in a granite wall and took out a small box. At the press of the button, the door opened.

Inside was a work bench strewn with robot parts. Tools lined a wall. Robots in various states of repair were separated into two piles. Books similar to the ones Aunt Ruby showed me in the desert house were neatly stacked on shelves. A bright light shone from the ceiling directly over the bench.

Green looked at the paper. "Your file says that you have experience in electronics. You'll take parts from scrap robots in that pile and place them on malfunctioning robots in the other. You'll sleep in this room. Food will be brought to you. This is a privileged position. Don't abuse it or you'll join the sludgers in the troughs. Repair three robots a day." Green left and sealed the door behind him.

A thin mattress with a blanket lay in one corner. A toilet and sink were in another. Except for the one door, there no exits. Two vents in the wall brought in air, but they were no wider than my fist.

My only hope might be to overpower whoever came to retrieve a repaired robot and make a run for one of the large pipes. Presumably, they led somewhere out of the cave. I might also be able to find the tunnels where Aunt Ruby hid in and make contact with her people.

I took a robot from the malfunctioning stack and placed it on the work bench, noted the model number and retrieved the appropriate drawing from one of the books. It was a struggle to recall the electronics I learned from my childhood hobby as I read the notes. One had the word *Diagnostics* with an arrow that pointed to a spot on a circuit board. I removed a plate on the robot's body and saw the small spot. When pressed, a voice came from the robot. "Malfunction. Left tread sensor inoperative. Replace."

I removed a cover on the left tread and looked at the schematics. I found what I thought was a sensor. It took some time to go through the stack of scrap robots before I found another with the same tread model. I removed the sensor and inserted it into the good robot. It snapped in place.

When I pressed the *Diagnose* button again, the robot responded, "All systems operative."

Soon after, the door to my workshop made a whoosh sound. I looked up to see a woman with a clipboard and two guards. I couldn't overpower them all.

The woman walked in. "One third daily quota reached." She directed the robot to follow her and the two men out of the shop. The door closed behind them.

I put my head in my hands. There was no escape. Unlike with Aunt Ruby, there weren't even other prisoners to organize. I would have to pace myself and not repair robots too fast or they might increase my quota.

CHAPTER SIX

Months passed. Each day, I repaired three robots, never four. I built a clock and calendar out of the remains of a music composing robot to gauge when I should complete the third one.

It became easier to understand the drawings and swap out parts. This gave me a strange sense of satisfaction. Still, I knew I could never make true repairs or build a robot from scratch. I did have time for brief conversations with some of the more intelligent AI robots before they were retrieved and returned to duty.

One morning, I picked up another damaged robot and brought it to the bench. The model number seemed familiar. I studied the schematics and realized they were the same drawings Aunt Ruby showed me. I recognized the door opening unit. This time, I understood how it functioned.

The unit was not large. It could fit neatly in my hand. I needed a low-level power supply. Any standard one would give off an electrical signal sensors might detect.

Then, I remembered the Cdisk Jenkins gave me. It was powered by the heat of my fingers. No one bothered to take it away.

Fifteen minutes after my next meal was delivered,

I removed the Cdisk from my pocket and pressed it against the door opener. The microvolts of energy were just enough to open the door to the workshop.

I slipped outside as my heart raced. Large boulders littered the cavern floor. Men and women ambled about. Some carried broken robot parts. Others dragged sleds filled with boxes.

I came to a hydroponic greenhouse. Lights blazed inside. I peered from around a boulder and watched people tend plants. I couldn't tell if the food they grew was for consumption above or below ground.

A man dragged a sled across the floor. He reached the boulder next to me, stumbled and fell.

I crawled across the empty space and felt for a pulse. He was dead.

A voice from a loud speaker said, "Escaped prisoner. Lone man. Search near robot repair shop. Kill on sight."

People with batons came out of the greenhouse.

I pushed the dead man's body under an overhang of the boulder, placed the harness around myself and dragged the sled. The weight was immense. I wondered how the starved man had moved it at all.

A uniformed woman with a baton rushed past me. I had no idea where to go and was afraid I could be stopped and interrogated at any moment.

I skirted the shadows of the cavern until I came to one of the U-shaped troughs. It led to a sewer pipe three times the height of a person. The stench was wretched.

There were no guards around. I entered the trough and moved down the flow. People pushed muck with their hands and arms. Some wore shreds of clothes. Others worked naked. All were gaunt. Their bodies and hair were encased in filth.

I covered myself with slime and moved muck forward with the others as I inched toward the pipe. Once inside, some turned around and headed back to the trough. I continued on with those who remained.

A uniformed guard walked down the pipe.

I kept my gaze down like the others.

He stopped in front of me. "You're well-fed for a sludger." He raised his baton for a strike.

My reaction was purely instinctual, born out of years of police training and experience. I jammed my shoulders into his ankles.

He fell forward face down.

Then, I did something outside of my training I never thought I'd do. I jumped on his back and pushed his face into the liquid muck.

He flailed with his baton and tried to turn over.

I bore down on his neck with all my weight and kept his mouth and nose buried.

After a few moments, his body went limp. I waited a little while longer before I released my grip, then quickly stripped off his uniform so he wouldn't be easily identified and left him naked in the mud. I buried his belongings under muck and ran down the pipe.

There were fewer and fewer workers until I was alone. I walked for hours through the horrid stench. Every hundred steps or so I looked over my shoulder but could see no one.

At last, the pipe ended at a grate. Beyond was a deserted beach. Muck poured out of the pipe, dropped down to the beach and continued across the sand and into the ocean. I activated the door mechanism and the grate swung open.

After I jumped down to the beach, the grate closed behind me. The screech of sea birds called overhead. The fresh scent of salt water filled my nostrils.

Back up the pipe was everything I'd ever known. It had been a good life. I was happy. Since my incarceration, I only thought of survival and bottled all my feelings. I hadn't thought of everything I'd lost.

With the immediate stress and trauma gone, all the suppressed emotions flooded out. I dropped to my knees and gave a guttural cry while I pounded my fists against the sand. "Lies. All lies. A lifetime of lies."

Sobs overtook me. Thoughts of my mother, my father, and all the friends I ever knew rose up within me. They were still caught in the lies. I screamed louder until my breath became ragged and my throat sore.

I sat there as the waves crashed on the shore and the sun set over the mountain behind me. Even in the dark, I didn't move. My mind was devoid of thoughts.

When I looked up, there was no moon, but uncounted pinpoints of stars shined overhead, more marvelous than they had been at the motel.

Away from the ocean was a clump of grass. I dropped to the ground and must have fallen right to sleep because when I opened my eyes again it was morning.

After I stripped off my clothes and shoes, I washed them in the ocean using sand as a detergent substitute. Then, I bathed myself using sand to scrub away the last of the filth from the drain pipe.

There was a stream of fresh water just up from the coast but nothing to eat. For the first time in my life, I felt the pangs of hunger.

I walked south down the beach for what seemed like hours. A retro-resort appeared on the horizon. After getting closer, I saw it was set in the 17th century with a pirate theme.

At the first restaurant I came to, I gorged myself. The server gladly accepted the Cdisk. Everyone must have thought I was in closed mode and respected the privacy.

After eating, I purchased new clothes and shoes, then blended into the crowd and contemplated what to do next. My stomach still felt hungry. I picked up several packets of wafers, ate two and stuffed the rest in a pocket.

My options seemed bleak. I could try to return home and let everyone think I was in closed mode, but I realized they now thought I was dead. My apartment was certainly reassigned. Without The Connection I couldn't even get food.

If I reached Jenkins in person, I might be able to convince him I was wrongly accused. He always liked me and might plead my case with his superiors. The police force is a close-knit family. If Jenkins got enough support, the directors might be convinced to let me return.

Perhaps my link could be modified to restrict all transmission concerning the incident with Aunt Ruby so no one else was exposed. The timing would be hard. I'd have to sneak back into the city undetected and get Jenkins to go into closed mode so he wouldn't transmit my presence. If he was unable or unwilling to help, I was convinced he would allow me to leave without turning me in.

I could try to wander the world and stay incognito. There were thousands of retro-resorts, each with a different theme. Everyone would think I was in closed mode as they did in the desert. The Cdisk would provide all the wealth I needed. I could live a good life, yet I'd be a hunted man. The idea didn't settle with me. Besides, somewhere out there someone from my past might recognize me.

I needed a safe place, like the house in the desert where I met Aunt Ruby. A place where no one would look for me. No matter what choice I made, I needed to get away from people who were linked.

The memory of the piece of paper I found in Philip Santos' room came to mind. 356 Chelsea Street.

I rented an air car with the Cdisk and wished I still had the thim. By asking careful questions, I discovered the resort was at the base of a mountain next to the gulf north of the Caribbean in the old nation of Mexico.

Once in the air, I filed a flight plan for Paris. When the car was over the horizon, I opened a maintenance hatch in the ceiling, shorted out the location transponder and took manual control. Central Control would know the transponder failed, but would either think I'd crashed in the water or the car was still en route across the Atlantic Ocean with a defective transponder.

The flight was exhausting. With the transponder disabled all the navigation instruments had to be controlled manually. The effort exhausted me. I used a few high- level maps for major metropolitan centers to locate Glendale and Chelsea Street in the old state of California near Los Angeles.

The sun was my only guide. I turned the aircar west until I came to the Pacific Ocean where I headed north. It took all my concentration as I was forced to dodge robot craft and retain a low altitude to avoid detection.

I reached Los Angeles sooner than I'd anticipated. The built in maps only showed the more prominent streets. Luckily, Chelsea was among them.

I landed the aircar in Glendale on Chelsea a block away from number 356 and got out. Hard rain began to fall. I hadn't thought to purchase a coat at the resort.

This neighborhood was one of the places deemed too uneconomical to redevelop. The street consisted of single-family dwellings with yards around them. Paint peeled on the sides of buildings. Windows were broken. Some of the walls and roofs were caved in from a lack of maintenance.

The area was supposed to be deserted. I was surprised when a small girl dressed in rags emerged from between two houses.

She eyed me for a moment, then approached. "You got food?"

I smiled at her, reached into my pocket and handed her a wafer.

She snatched it away and ran back toward one of the houses. "He's got food."

Two dozen boys and girls no older than twelve swarmed out into the street. They carried sticks and clubs.

I reached into my pocket, threw the rest of the wafers onto the street and ran.

The children stopped to pick up the food.

I was shocked by the conditions. The city where I lived was bright and spacious. No one was hungry. My education taught me everywhere in the world was the same.

I found 356 Chelsea and knocked on the door.

A man opened it. "Yes?".

"Aunt Ruby sent me. I've got something on my mind and she said you could help."

The man stood at the door and looked me over. "I'm sorry. There's no one here by that name." He waited another moment. "You're soaked. Won't you come in to dry off?"

It was a trap, of course, but I had no other options. "Thank you. It is wet out here."

Once inside, the door was slammed and the man pointed a projectile pistol at me. Another man and a woman stood in a hallway.

The man with the gun said, "Stay where you are. Kate, check the scanners."

Kate headed for a door. "Yes, Sid."

I put my hands in the air. "No one followed me. The transponder in the car is disabled. It's a block down the street."

Sid pushed the gun into my face. "Shut up until I ask you a question. Sit down on the floor. Larry, check out the aircar."

Larry went out the door.

Sid stood over me until Kate returned. "The area is clean."

Larry came inside, "The transponder's disabled as he said."

Sid looked down at me. "How did you know this address?"

"My name is George Chen. I was a police detective. My last case was to track down a disconnect. I saw the address on a piece of paper."

Sid looked up to his companions. "Close down. We'll tie him up and leave him for his friends."

"Please, listen to me. No one else saw the address. The paper dissolved in my hand, and no one even wanted to hear my report. I'm an outcast now. The directors banished me underground the same as Aunt Ruby. She'll know who I am. Let me speak to her."

Sid hesitated.

Kate said, "Kill him. He's seen our faces."

My mind raced. "Would you be like the directors?"

Sid studied me for a moment. "Get up."

I was escorted to another room.

Few would have recognized the object I saw there. I learned about ancient communication devices at the academy. It was a computer monitor with a video camera on top.

The screen glowed and Aunt Ruby's face appeared. "Hello, George."

Her image was the most reassuring thing I'd seen since my abduction. My eyes teared over. "I didn't want to believe it. I couldn't. I thought you were lying to me and when I met the directors I was certain they'd apprehend you."

I put my hands over my face. "Instead, they condemned me to the pit and I knew who was lying."

She nodded. "I understand. I didn't want to believe it either."

I forced myself to calm down. Though I was still shaking, I was able to tell her the whole story. I felt lighter, though the sense of terror and injustice was still there.

Again, I thought of my friends and family, the life

now lost, the dreams and hopes I'd held. I saw the faces of my father and mother in my mind. I saw my apartment. I saw my friends.

Could I go back? Would I be accepted?

I also saw the cavern beneath the Earth, the corpses in the sewer and the little girl in rags who begged for food on the street.

My entire life was made of lies. I'd lived in ignorant bliss and asked myself if I could unknow what I now realized.

My pulse raced. They still might think a former police detective a liability to their cause. "I considered running from retro-resort to retro-resort with the Cdisk, then realized I couldn't turn my back on humanity. After the house was raided in the desert, I didn't know how to find you. Then I remembered Chelsea Street."

All the possibilities ran through my head until there was only one answer.

I looked into Aunt Ruby's eyes. "I want to join your movement. I know things that can help. Let me help look for the honey flowers."

Aunt Ruby took a long time to reply. "Many disconnects have found us. Most live quiet lives analyzing the meager information we've gathered. Field work is dangerous. Honeybees are captured and killed by the secret security force. If they find you again, you won't just be killed. You'll suffer torture in revenge."

"I've faced horrors I never imagined. My police training instilled service and duty. I protected people every day. I just didn't understand who the real criminals are. Whatever the risk, I can't walk away."

After several seconds, she leaned forward with a

smile. "Courage and commitment are the greatest requirements to be a Honeybee. Welcome to the resistance, George."

Dreamglass

R ain drenched my body as I lay in the mud and listened to the approach of the mounted soldiers. No moon shone that night. Still, I knew Duke Bersan and his men would find me, and then I would die.

I forced myself up and ran through a thicket of woods to a road worn by wagon wheels. Tacked to a tree was a poster with a sketch of my face. Below it was written, "Wanted. Anar Varolta, thief from the Barony of Lasta. One gold piece reward."

The Duke was a wizard. He now tracked me through the enchanted dagger I stole from his castle. I drew it from my belt. To the eye it was plain with a polished wood hilt, straight blade, and simple brass pommel. Yet to hold that dagger, to feel it in your hand, was to know perfection. It fit perfectly in my grasp with the blade balanced for fighting or throwing, and the ability to cut through flesh or wood or armor with the same ease. Bersan seized it as plunder after ransacking the Barony of Lasta a decade before.

A clink of livery sounded. Through the pounding torrent, the outline of a farmer's cart approached. I stumbled into thick brush with no idea of the direction I took.

A month before, I sat warm and dry on a bench in Baron Genla Lasta's gardens next to his daughter, Meleray.

Doubt filled my mind as I looked to the ground. "Sons of first ministers don't marry daughters of barons."

She took my hand. "I am free to marry whomever I choose. I choose you."

Her touch warmed me, yet I shivered. "I'm not worthy. I've never seen battle, never proved my courage. The baron won't consent."

A smile came to her lips. "I consent."

"I would degrade you in court."

She stood and drew me to my feet. "I love you, Anar. Do you love me?"

Tears came to my eyes. "I have loved you for years."

She put her arms around me. "Then nothing else matters."

We rocked together under the springtime sun. Still, a pit formed in my stomach. "I will prove my love." I stepped back. "Give me a task. No matter the danger, it will be done."

"What task could I ask but to have you by my side?"

I thought for a moment. "I will retrieve your father's enchanted dagger from Duke Bersan. That will prove I'm brave and worthy."

"No one cares about that old thing."

"Your father's reputation was soiled. I will give him reason to praise me."

Meleray shook her head, her face clouded. "Don't talk of such foolish things, even in jest. Berson is vile and cruel. He would kill you for sport."

My gaze narrowed. "I am no fool. I do this for you."

"I didn't call you a fool. Don't put yourself in danger for a meaningless object."

I stepped away from her. "You think me weak."

She shook her head. "Listen to yourself. What has come over you?"

"Nothing has come over me. I've made up my mind. You will not marry a coward."

A cloud covered the sun. Meleray turned and ran off as she cried.

A crack of thunder startled me and cut off the vision. I returned to reality, and in doing so, remembered again the words that marred our parting. She despised the quest. As I rode away from the barony, I feared she despised me too. That would change, I told myself, when I presented the dagger to her father. She would see I was right.

The brush rustled. I tried to stand but fell back into the mud. My fingers tightened around the hilt of the dagger. I might die this night, but I would not die alone.

A man's face appeared. He was fat, with a wide nose and slate gray eyes. The skin on his face was wrinkled with age. He wore a brown woolen traveling cloak with a hood drawn over his head. My fingers tightened on the knife, then my strength failed and the dagger dropped from my grasp.

The man picked it up, tucked it into a pouch, and bent over to lift me from the mire. The driving rain fell in sheets as he carried me through the woods. I couldn't tell how long we traveled, though I recall the sounds of the horses moving away from us. Drained by my flight, I fell asleep as he carried me.

When I awoke, I lay on a cot in one corner of a cave. Woolen blankets were wrapped about my body. A fire blazed in a hearth carved into the stone wall. On a chair next to the fire my soiled clothes dried.

The old man stirred something in a cauldron. When he saw I was awake, he spooned some into a wooden bowl and brought it to me. I started to sit up, but he waved me back down, then spoke in a deep, resonant voice. "Stay still, lad. Turn your head and I'll hold the spoon."

The steaming liquid brought warm comfort as it slid down my throat. The cold of the rain storm, the ache of the climb, the terror of pursuit, all receded to the back of my mind. The old man tucked the covers around me. "Rest now. All will be well in the morning."

I turned my head and watched him walk to the cave entrance. The rain still poured as the old man went out into the storm. He raised his right hand over his head and waved his wrist to and fro. A shimmer formed above him, like a gossamer canopy, and the water was diverted as he walked.

I feared my mind was hallucinating and wondered if the cave was an illusion and I still laid in the mud and rain. My eyes closed and I fell fast asleep.

I awoke in terror and confusion. Where was I? What had happened? Was I in Bersan's dungeon? My cries echoed in the cave as I tried to rise.

Gentle hands guided my shoulders back to the cot. "Easy, lad. You're safe, but you've taken much hurt. How you managed to get this far, I don't know. You need rest."

His pudgy, wrinkled face smiled down on me. He raised a cup of water to my parched lips.

It tasted better than the finest wine. "Thank you. Thank you for everything. I must warn you, though, you're in grave danger for as long as I'm under your roof."

He looked up at the rock ceiling of the cave and smiled. "Well, it's not exactly a roof, but I thank you for your concern. Still, I don't think your enemies will find you here. Few know this country well, and fewer yet, this cave."

I should have suspected this old man. A bounty lay on my head, enough to make any farmer or herdsman rich for a lifetime. Still, there was something about him that refuted caution.

I took another sip of water and settled back against the pillow. "There is more at work here, kind sir, than is apparent. Magic tracks me, and unless I should abandon the quest which has brought me here, I shall surely be captured. I am Anar Varolta of Lasta, and have recovered an enchanted dagger stolen by Duke Bersan."

A part of me expected him to run and alert the Duke. Instead, he placed his right hand on his heart and bowed low. "Then you must be the son of First Minister Varolta. I travelled to Lasta in my youth and remember your name when you were but an infant. It is my honor to have you in my home. I am Beku Tafes. You are welcome to stay as long as you desire."

I tried to give a quick, concise explanation of myself, but as I talked, I found I wished to say more and more to Beku Tafes. Words poured out of me—hopes, desires, fears. Things I hadn't said to any other person. As I did, a feeling of lightness swelled in my chest.

At last, I told him of Meleray, the source of my quest, and how she loathed me for taking it up. He listened without interruption.

As my tale ended, he brought more soup. "Rest now, lad. You need time to heal. Be assured this is a safe place for you."

I drank the soup and fell quickly asleep. When I stirred again I knew many hours had passed, for the candle at my bedside was burned halfway down.

At first I thought I was alone. Then, in a corner of the cave, I saw Beku Tafes approach a pile of boxes and crates.

He didn't notice me, but stared intently at one particular chest. With a sigh, he reached out, removed it from the pile, and sat with it on the floor. His hands trembled as he fingered the dust covered lid.

With deliberation, he lifted the top and took out a round, cut crystal attached to a purple ribbon. The crystal glowed. He held it in his hands as his jaw quivered and his brow furrowed. For an instant, he appeared young and strong. The perception faded to reveal a tired, old man whose eyes were filled with tears. He returned the crystal to the case, then shoved it under others in the pile.

Whatever it was he saw, I couldn't begin to imagine. Still, a sense of deep loss came to me and I found myself weeping for Beku Tafes, though I had no idea why.

I slept till late afternoon when the sun outside the cave was low in the sky. Beku Tafes was nowhere to be seen. My head still hurt, but I found I was able to stand and move around with care.

My stomach grumbled. I went to the cauldron for some more soup. It was empty, so I walked towards the back of the cave in search of food. As I passed the boxes, I noticed the small chest.

An overpowering desire filled me with the urge to look into the crystal. It was as if a voice shouted in my head, "Hold me." I fought the command, yet found my fingers wrapped around the chest. Like a marionette, I opened the lid and took out the clear crystal.

At first, I saw nothing. Relief flooded me. I could put the box back before Beku Tafes returned. Then, an image congealed in the crystal. In it, a man stood on a hillside above an ocean cove. He was tall and strong. I recognized him as Beku Tafes, though thinner and younger. A woman stood at his side. She was nearly as tall as him with long dark hair and hazel eyes. At their feet two children played and laughed. The woman took his arm in hers and smiled at him. He placed his hand over hers and smiled in return. The image remained for a moment, then faded and the crystal was once again clear.

"How dare you!" Beku Tafes' angry voice filled the cave. "You fool. The magic locked in those boxes could turn you to stone, rip your body asunder, burn you to ash."

Beku Tafes charged forward, snatched the crystal from my grasp and held it against his chest. His eyes bored into me.

I flinched, expecting a blow.

His whole body shook as he took short, rasping breaths. The gasps eased. His shoulders slumped, and he turned to stare at the hearth in silence.

I was overwhelmed with guilt. "I don't know what came over me. I just had to see, I don't know why. I've betrayed your hospitality and shall leave at once." I walked towards the cave entrance. My head became dizzy and I fell to one knee.

Beku Tafes was at my side in an instant. "Come now, lad. Back to the cot. You're not in any condition to leave, and I'm not of a mind to throw you out." He was no longer the tired old man. A mask descended, the veneer of one who is always in control. Yet I could see it was a pretense and he still hurt beneath the act.

He guided me back to bed and covered me with a blanket. Then he brought a chair over and sat next to me. Neither of us said anything for a long time as we watched the flames in the hearth.

Unable to keep the silence, I said, "Master Tafes, I feel quite terrible about this."

"Don't blame yourself, lad. The call of a dreamglass is hard to ignore. I have certainly heard it enough."

"Is it a memory locked away magically?" I slapped my hands over my mouth. "Oh, I didn't mean to pry."

He laughed. "No need to be sorry. I awoke it when I opened the chest last night. It had been asleep for many years, it's voice only a faint whisper. I guess it was your story that brought it to mind, the woman you plan to marry and fear you've lost. At any rate, I thought to have just a small look."

"But what is it?"

"It's a wish, caught in crystal forever. It's not a thing that ever happened, rather a desire for how a person wants things to be. It is my dreamglass. My wish."

"Then the woman, the children, they're not real?"

"The woman is. Her name was Evesana. The children are what might have been. I loved Evesana as I was certain I could love no other."

I thought about Meleray. When I rode from the castle, she grabbed my leg and begged me to abandon the quest. When I continued on, she shouted, "Is it me you love, or your own pride?"

Hollowness washed through my body then. The retrieval of the dagger was the price I set upon myself to wed her. How could she love me and not understand?

As I sat in the cave, I wondered if Evesana gave Beku Tafes an impossible choice. "Master, what happened to the woman?"

He shifted in his chair. "I was a young and ambitious wizard. She was tall, and lovely, and smart. Her wit lit up the room, which is why I fell in love with her. We went on long walks and discussed the world. Once, I gathered meadow flowers and set them to light magically as a garland. She was delighted."

His eyes opened as a smile formed on his lips. "One day, I vowed to make her the most wonderful gift to show my feelings. My mind with filled with images of extravagant boats and castles we could live in forever. None seemed great enough for her."

The eyes frowned and his smile evaporated. "Then, I did a foolish thing. I made a dreamglass and filled it with all my love for her."

"Master Tafes, if it was filled with love how could its creation be foolish?"

His voice became a near whisper. "I sat in my rooms with the dreamglass held close as I fell immersed into the image. I no longer walked with her in the gardens or spoke with her of the world. She pleaded with me to cast it aside and embrace her. Instead, I left with my magic to spend all my time with the dreamglass uninterrupted. Now, it holds me. I can't leave its presence. I can't even unmake or destroy it."

I felt the chill of the cave run to my bones. Was I now consumed by the quest to retrieve the dagger? It was to be an expression of love. The quest now took on a life of its own. I went to the table and stroked my fingers along the weapon's hilt. My hand tingled as I drew it away. I thought I heard a voice say, "Hold me."

In the middle of the night, Beku Tafes shook me awake. "Quick, dress yourself. We must flee before they find the cave."

"What's wrong?"

"My fault. An old fool, that's what I am. All that self-abasing pity last night. I let the magical shield falter. Bersan is coming."

I dressed while Beku Tafes hunted through his chests. "We'll need a few things. Can't let them discover the cave and let the boxes fall into the Duke's hands. Hurry now. We have to lay a well-scented trail on the other side of the hill."

He took out a metal breastplate. It was embossed with the image of a leaping lion. "Here, help me on with this. Careful. I know it would fit better were there fifty pounds less of me. For now, just let out the straps on the sides." He brought out a metal cap and a sword.

"I should wear the armor and wield the sword, Master Tafes. I'm a strong young man."

"And I'm a fat old one. Yes, I know. But the armor is enchanted. Don't worry. There is much power in this sword and armor. I complain too much, for in truth it's as light as a feather for me, and the sword wields itself at my command. Come now. We must hurry."

Lastly, he opened the chest and placed the dreamglass in a pouch.

We ran from the cave and charged up a slope. At the crest, I paused for a moment. A grassy hillside stretched out before us. In the distance was an ocean cove.

We descended a trail. Beku Tafes inspected the path. "This will do to start the chase." He closed his eyes and recited a low chant. His eyes opened again. "Come. They will now follow this trail and miss the cave. We must reach the water before sundown. I'll cast a spell to make them think you've escaped across the sea back to Lasta."

The sun was high overhead when we paused for a rest. Beku Tafes retrieved a mold of cheese and some bread from a sack. "Eat. We need strength if we're to reach our goal."

As I ate, I thought about the dreamglass. It had been on my mind all morning. I tried to remember if Meleray ever looked at me the way the woman in the glass had to Beku Tafes.

It was late afternoon when we reached the beach. Beku Tafes walked across the sand. "Wait. I must rest to perform the spell."

Before we could sit, three mounted riders burst through the brush behind us. Five more followed.

I drew the dagger.

Beku Tafes pushed me back towards the sea. "Stand clear, lad. That blade would have little effect here."

He bound forward like a young warrior. His armor gleamed in the sunlight as he swung the sword with skill and practice, sometimes stabbing, sometimes slashing. Blows of mace and sword and axe crashed against his cap and breastplate. They had no effect against the magic armor. Beku Tafes' enchanted sword cut through the enemies armor like cloth. Blood stained the sand as men fell from their horses. Six more mounted soldiers came out of the forest and charged Beku Tafes. Each met with a swift death.

The brush parted. Duke Bersan rode onto the beach followed by ten mounted guards. He was a gaunt figure. A twisted smile came to his lips as he raised a twig-like finger towards us. "Beku Tafes. I thought you dead. Yet here you stand defending this whelp. No doubt your hoard of magic is nearby as well. This will be a most profitable day indeed. Stand aside, old man. You can lead me to your treasure soon enough. First, I want this prince and the dagger he stole."

Beku Tafes raised his sword. "I do not think so Duke Bersan. Long you have studied the arts, but not nearly as long as me. Depart this place and you take your life. Stand, and you die as these other fools have."

The Duke spit on the sand. "We shall see who is the fool, old man." He clapped his hands together. The sand in front of him rose up like a great wave and shot towards us.

Beku Tafes scribed the tip of his sword across the beach in front of him. The wave collapsed back into the sand. "You shall have to do much better than that."

Duke Bersan dismounted and took a ring from his finger. It was gold with a large brown gem set into it. He uttered a shrill incantation and threw the ring into the sand. A flash nearly blinded me.

When my eyes recovered, a demon stood over the ring. It was as tall as three men. Sword length teeth bristled from a lipless mouth. It walked on three legs and had four arms. Each ended in talons.

With a single swipe, it knocked Beku Tafes aside. The talons dented his breastplate. Beku Tafes pushed himself up and stabbed the demon in one leg. The hellish monster bellowed and kicked at the old man. He was knocked across the sand to lay motionless face down. The demon advanced.

I ran forward. Beku Tafes was still alive, though he breathed in shallow gasps. The demon bore down on us. Dagger in hand, I prepared to meet death.

Bersan spoke another incantation. The demon stopped its advance. The Duke repeated the spell. This time the demon turned and growled. Bersan spoke a third time. The monster covered its ears and walked back to the ring on the beach. When it stood over the gem, a flash of light exploded and the creature was once more sealed away.

The Duke retrieved his ring and strode towards us. His soldiers rode up behind.

Beku Tafes stirred. He chanted a spell, raised his sword, and pointed it towards the advancing enemy.

Bersan's eyes widened. He dropped to the sand and shouted for the men behind him to get down.

The warning came too late for the guards. The tip of Beku Tafes' sword glowed as bright as the sun. A ball of fire shot from the weapon. It ran over Bersan's prone body and engulfed the mounted troops. The inferno consumed men and horses.

Only the Duke and his mount survived. He stood, his eyes narrowed, his teeth bared. He took out a small, red ball and held it overhead.

I grasped the enchanted dagger and took a fighting stance.

Bersan laughed. "Fool. No weapon can touch me. I am sealed in a magical shield more potent than this old man's armor."

I look down to Beku Tafes' shattered body. A shout erupted from my throat. I threw the dagger with all my strength. The magical blade struck the sphere. It fell from the Duke's grasp and struck the ground at his feet.

A thunder crack rolled across the beach. Bersan screamed as his body began to turn to stone. It started with his legs and moved up towards his chest. He pleaded for me to kill him, to end the torment. I could neither move nor look away, being both fascinated and revolted by the transforming magic.

The screams stopped when his mouth became stone. Still, his eyes looked out in horror until they too were transformed to rock. Bersan's grotesque image sat on the beach for only a moment before fine cracks appeared across the surface. The horrific statue crumbled in on itself and became dust that was blown away by the sea breeze.

I ran to Beku Tafes. He opened his eyes a slit. "Fine job, lad. Showed them a thing or two, didn't we?" He coughed and blood foamed on his lips.

"Don't talk, master. I'll get a horse and take you back to the cave."

"No time. I'm dying, lad." His breath slowed. "Take the sword. At dawn hold it aloft. The blade will soak up the rising sun's power. Point it at a target and command the sword to let loose the fire. You can do this but once a day. It will also cut through any armor. You will be a one-man legion with it."

He coughed again. "Use a fireball to seal the cave. The secrets within are too powerful. If another like Duke Bersan should find them, there would be no end to the evil."

"Master, can't I help? Can't you heal yourself?"

He shook his head. "The magic's gone. The demon drained most of it. I used the last to mend my arm so I could raise the sword."

His voice became desperate. He pulled the dreamglass from the pouch and held it to his chest. "Don't make the same mistake I did. Dreams can smother you if you don't make them happen. I became obsessed with one ideal and trapped myself in longing."

His eyes closed as his breath slowed until it stopped. The dreamglass fell to the sand, then melted. Beku Tafes was free at last.

The next morning, I rode the dead duke's horse back to the cave. Inside, I gathered food and water skins, along with a shovel. Once outside, I sealed its magical treasures from the world as Beku Tafes requested, all except the sword.

I mounted and rode back to the beach to bury Beku Tafes.

Afterwards, I sat in the sand and stared at the waves. The woman I loved was across that sea. Did she still love the man who sat on this shore? Beku Tafes drove Evesana away. The image of riding alone from Meleray's castle as she pleaded with me to stay bit into me.

The dagger sat in my hand, the bride piece. With a hard toss, I cast it into the ocean. As it sank, a weight lifted.

I mounted the horse and set off for a port to take me back to Lasta with the hope I'd grown up and Meleray would forgive me.

ABOUT THE AUTHOR

David A. Wimsett writes novels and short stories as well as articles, columns and blogs for corporations, magazines, newspapers and online platforms. He's appeared on radio and television talk shows and on stage as an actor in musicals, comedies and dramas.

He worked in computer software and hardware for decades and wrote fractal programs to generate random landscapes on computer screens.

He became a single parent in his twenties and both raised and guided his son into adulthood.

His works entertain and raise questions through engaging stories with strong, complex characters of diverse genders, orientations, colors and ethnic backgrounds who face challenges in their lives as they grow and have the opportunity to examine themselves and their place in the world.

Mr. Wimsett is a member of the Writers' Union of Canada and the Canadian Freelance Guild.

He lives in a rural town near the sea. His author's website is https://www.davidawimsett.com.